DREAMLAND
and other stories

Jan Mazzoni

Many of these stories have appeared in magazines in the UK
and around the world

Front cover photo: Laura Thayer @ ciaoamalfi

© 2018 Jan Mazzoni

CONTENTS

JOURNEY'S END
AT THE BAR
EARTHQUAKES AND MINOR SHOCKS
LIMONCELLO
THE ART OF MAKING SPAGHETTI
RAVELLO
THE WOMAN WHO LOVED TO PLAY GAMES
DROUGHT
WHATEVER MAKES YOU HAPPY
LEARNNG TO SWIM
THE SILLIEST OF THINGS
DREAMLAND
THE SWIFTS OF AMALFI
POSTCARDS
FOR THE LAST TIME

PREFACE

IT'S THE 1980s...

Italy's Amalfi Coast has long been popular with the jet set, those who are 'in the know'- film and rock stars, politicians, poets and artists who scour the world for the most beautiful places, always one step ahead of the crowd. But in the 1980s the trickle of visitors turned into a flood. Cheap air flights, package tours that took the fear out of venturing somewhere where they spoke a different language, a growing interest in foreign foods – all reasons why visitors to this stunning part of southern Italy were suddenly on the increase.

Gradually the trail blazers moved on in search of somewhere new. But no-one really noticed.

From a 1983 Travel Brochure

The world-famous Amalfi Drive follows the coast between Sorrento and Salerno, 30 miles of snake like twists and sudden sharp curves that take the breath away. Below is the sparkling turquoise Tyrrhenian sea, above tower dramatic mountains often topped with wisps of cloud. And along the coast a scattering of villages where you can pause, take a deep jasmine-scented breath, and then step outside your everyday life into another world.

Sergio, tour bus driver

Si, e vero. We Italian men love the women. *Perche no*? And the women who come here, they love us. They are bored with their husbands. We are real men. So of course we flirt with them. We give flowers, say pretty things. Sometimes we make love with them. Sure, we have wives but they are doing what a woman is born to do – they cherish *i bambini*, they cook the pasta for when we come home, tired, hungry. They know we will always come home. These silly tourists, they mean nothing to us. *Niente.* But *certo*, we enjoy. So in the end, everyone happy, yes?

Joy and misery are two sides of the same coin.

JOURNEY'S END

If it was good enough for John Steinbeck, Alberto Moravia, for Tennessee Williams, it would do for them. Such literary giants had standards. Besides, it sounded so beautiful, so improbable. They felt they already knew it: Judy describing its tumble of unending steps, its white piazza where boys played football beneath a statue of Christ, the tiny beach that would be empty now, ironed flat by heavy winter seas the colour of metal, reading from a guidebook as the bus snaked cautiously along the rain-wet road. Pete listened, nodded, smiled inwardly at Judy's excitement. She found everything exciting.

Even after being with her constantly for a hundred and sixty-three days (she didn't know he was counting, of course), still he wasn't used to it.

It was dark when the bus abandoned them outside a bar, its windows steamed up so that all they could see were vague shapes, sexless, ageless. It looked crowded.

"Hungry?"

"Starving."

"OK. In we go."

The mumble of conversation faded as the locals, mostly men, turned to look at the tall pale couple in jeans, the girl with yellow hair sliding out from under an old fedora, the boy bearded, both stooped under the weight of rucksacks. As the door swung closed behind them sentences were completed, laughter resumed, a game of cards suddenly won with shouts of disbelief. Someone moved over, chairs were brought.

The smoke was thick as the froth on the *cappuccinos* Pete balanced back to the table. He returned to the counter for squares of pizza so hot they burnt his fingers through the paper napkins, but still they ate them quickly. Without speaking, he went back for more.

"D'you think John Steinbeck drank in this bar?" He reached across and wiped a dab of tomato sauce from Judy's chin.

"He probably sat on this very chair, it's old enough."

"Bet Tennessee Williams did."

"I thought he drank gin in his hotel room. Wouldn't come out. Didn't someone tell us that?"

"Probably. He died in a hotel room, just a few years ago, I remember that."

"So sad."

"So stupid to waste your talent like he did."

They lowered their voices, heads bent close, not wanting to stand out. There were no tourists here now, not in winter. Not that they would have described themselves as tourists. Wanderers, maybe. Drifters. Seekers, though neither of them could have defined exactly what they were seeking.

The door opened again. Two men and a boy entered, wrapped in blankets the colours of winter, browns and white, fringed in grey, a smell of goats about them. Their hair was long, matted; their eyes nervous and wild like those of a cornered animal. They stood and waited for silence, then began to play music, a strange sound, thin, harsh, on an instrument like bagpipes. A sound from another world, a time long past. Judy shivered without knowing why. When the music stopped one of the men walked silently amongst the tables, his hand extended. Not begging, not demanding. He simply held out his hand. Everyone gave something; Pete dug deep into a pocket, dropped coins into the hand that was worn and polished, like seasoned wood. The man nodded.

As the musicians left, a television above the bar was switched on, as though to re-affirm the time and place. The normality of life.

"*I ciociari*," someone told them. "Shepherds. From up in the mountains." He spoke Italian, but they got the gist of what he said. "Some musicians, huh?" The man laughed, but not unkindly.

"Weird, wasn't it? But somehow... mesmerising." Judy knew Pete would agree with her. They felt the same about most things. She drained her cup, ran a finger around the inside.

"I hate to ask, Pete. But can we actually afford for pay for this?"

He pulled a face.

"You know we're going to have to give in sooner or later." He looked away. "We can't put it off any longer."

"I know. I just wish we didn't."

Judy caught hold of his hand, twined her fingers through his.

"Pete love, it really wasn't your fault. Stop blaming yourself. It happens all the time, overnight trains are full of thieves and murderers. It could have been worse. We could have had our throats cut."

She gave a small laugh.

"Besides, what are families for if not to be there when you need them."

A sudden gust of wind splattered rain against the windows that ran down in wobbly streaks. Pete shook himself.

"Anyway, first thing is to find somewhere to stay. By the time we're ready to move on we'll have some money, I promise. OK wait here, I'll ask at the bar.

The barman shook his head. It was Christmas. Most places would be closed. It used to be fashionable to spend Christmas at the village by the sea, the streets used to be crowded with visitors from the north, ladies in high heels and fur stole with small dogs under their arms, fat businessmen chewing cigars; there was music, dancing that went on into the night. But not anymore. Now the northern Italians stayed home or went up into the mountains or to Florida.

Still he asked around. Names were tossed back and forth, were scribbled on scraps torn from newspapers. A *pensione* that just might be open for guests, though wasn't *La Signora* expecting her family up from Sicily to stay? Houses with unused rooms someone might be willing to let for a few nights.

"*Grazie*. You're all very kind."

Pete stuffed the bits of paper inside his jacket, unable to read many of the scrawls, but grateful, warmed by their obvious concern. For strangers too.

"*Buon Natale,*" people called as they left.

Though the rain had stopped, the black, cold night was a shock; Judy caught hold of Pete's hand again and held on. The silence made it worse. Finding their way around was far from easy; there were few lights, even those from inside the houses reduced to faint slithers by thick shutters. Most doors were without numbers. In the end they knocked, held out the slips of paper, were directed this way and that. But still found no-one with a room for them, a bed for the night.

Rain from the rooftops had been channelled down onto the steps that served as streets so that many of them were like waterfalls; it was impossible to avoid wet feet, water seeping up so that their jeans stuck to their legs. Pete wanted so much for things to go right, wanted to shield Judy from such miseries as tramping night streets in search of a room. And things had been good to begin with, better than good. Wonderful. It had been all they'd expected of a trip to Europe.

Lately everything seemed to be going wrong. Maybe it was time to give up, go home.

"We'll find somewhere. Don't we always?" Judy was being positive.

It was late when they came to a house on the edge of the village, high up. They were breathless from the climb so that when a woman opened the door neither of them spoke immediately. The narrowness of the opening, her hand still on the door told of suspicion. With the light behind her they couldn't see her face.

"Sorry to disturb you this late. We're looking for a room for a night or two. Someone said you might..."

The woman looked from one to the other. Slowly she shook her head. Suddenly tears ran down Judy's rain-streaked face; she blinked hard, sniffed, furious with herself. It was so unlike her. Pete hugged her as they turned away.

The woman beckoned them back, left them standing in the narrow hallway where they dripped puddles onto the tiled floor. On a table was a glass dome inside which was a statue of the Madonna, a sepia photograph of a man in uniform, and a pink plastic pig. Pete gazed at it without speaking; Judy rummaged for something to blow her nose on. From the other room they could hear voices.

"Come."

She led them to a room, hardly more than a box room, its floor and walls crammed with bottles of tomatoes, pepperoni, with trays on which figs were drying, their skins crusty with sugar. The woman removed more boxes from the bed that stood against the wall, piled them in the hallway. She dug into a chest of drawers and pulled out blankets.

They tried to thank her but she, indicated the bathroom.

"*Buona notte,*" she muttered. She left them alone.

They slept without moving or dreaming, awoke to the familiar, delicious smell of coffee. During the night the rain had been blown out to sea; through the unshuttered window they could see a lemon sun floating in a watery blue sky that became, at some point, the sea, though it was hard to judge where one changed to the other. Below the house was an orange grove, fruit hanging from the branches, like baubles on a Christmas tree.

A brisk tap at the door.

The woman brought them a tray, on it two cups, a jug of coffee, another of milk, chunks of coarse bread. In a saucer, a pool of thick red jam. Still she didn't smile, simply said good morning, set down the tray. Smiling wasn't important; she'd saved their lives, no doubt about it. Now they luxuriated in breakfast in bed, propped up by fat pillows.

"So we'll telephone home this morning. Agreed?"

The subject was lurking like a large black spider on the ceiling.

"I guess. And they'll say: See, didn't we tell you? You two. It's time you grew up."

Judy joined in the imaginary conversation.

"Can't understand why you don't get married anyway. Get yourselves a nice little house, maybe with a pool."

"And put that degree to some use! If you're going to make a career for yourself, you'd better get on with it. Time and tide…"

"Oh and kids. You know, my mum accused me of denying her her right to be a grandma. Said I was being selfish."

"Just think of it: nappies and sleepless nights, prams in the hallway, Hershey bars melting in the bed."

"Hey, you know how I feel about sugar. I want my kids to keep their teeth, at least into their teens."

With a sigh Judy clambered over Pete to get out of bed, stood breathing deeply, stretched bare arms upwards. She started every day with ten minutes of yoga.

"I don't know, Jude. Maybe they're right. We've seen the places we planned on seeing, done most of the things. Maybe we should..."

"Should what?"

"Get married. Get a mortgage. Get jobs."

"Is that a proposal?" She was bent forwards grasping her ankles, head between her legs.

"D'you want it to be"

"No way." She said the words softly to make them less harsh. "I don't want to get married. Neither do you, remember? We agreed. We shook hands on it."

She twisted to look at Pete as he stared out of the window at a single gull dipping over the sea. His hair was long now, it curled over his shirt collar. She thought about trimming it, how it would feel between her fingers.

"You're right."

Judy straightened up, took a deep breath.

"God, I feel awful."

Making their way down to the village, to the bank, they picked lemons from behind a crumbling brick wall, Pete juggling with them so that soon a crowd of children gathered, watched in sombre silence, their dark eyes grown huge. When he stopped they simply stood and waited. He did cartwheels; they smiled. He jumped up onto the narrow wall, danced his way along it, pretended to fall then rolled over, jumped to his feet. They clapped, delighted. When he caught Judy's hand and ran off, the children followed.

"Never can resist an audience, can you?" Judy teased.

Her father answered the phone. His voice was warm. Of course he'd organise cash for them, no problem. Of course it wasn't their fault. It could have happened to anyone. He wished them a happy Christmas, said how they'd be missed by everyone. It's snowing, he said, settling too, a real New England Christmas. She felt a twinge of envy.

He told her he loved her, sent his best to Pete.

"God, he's so... so..." Judy slammed down the phone. Furious for all the things he hadn't said, didn't need to say.

"I'm sorry but I like your dad." Pete shrugged apologetically.

"Me too. When he's not being so smug anyway."

The man at the bank warned of a delay. This branch would be closed for the next few days; banks in the US too of course. He managed a small smile. They mustn't worry. They must enjoy themselves.

"*Buone feste,*" he said.

And yet still it didn't feel like Christmas. The village streets gave few hints of the season; one or two displays in shops no bigger than kiosks, a nativity scene set up in the window of a house where the donkey, a toy, towered like a monster mutant over the dwarfed figures of Mary and Joseph.

And it was warmer than they'd expected. They went down to the beach, sat on rocks. Phrase book in hand they worked out how to ask *La Signora* if they could stay until after Christmas, that they would pay her then, that they wouldn't get in the way at all. They'd promise.

"We can afford a drop of wine, can't we? Some bread and olives?"

"Sure we can. And can't imagine anyone objecting to us picking a couple of those oranges. I mean, they've got a whole grove of them, right?"

There was something satisfying about going without at Christmas. Certainly they'd miss the feasting, the once a year over-indulgence. But still, it wouldn't do them any harm to go without. There were other ways to celebrate besides eating too much and putting on weight, simpler ways. Like just being in the present moment, being together. Being there, in the place they'd dreamt about.

Being positive was easy in the sunshine, on the beach, the air sweet and sparkling as *acqua minerale*. Behind them, behind the village, there was snow on the mountain tops. The day stretched in front of them, all those empty hours waiting to be filled in whatever way they chose. Really, things weren't so bad.

La Signora agreed to their staying. At least, she nodded. Children appeared from somewhere, nudging each other, asking Pete and Judy questions they found it best to answer with smiles, touches. It was enough; children understand such things better than words.

"Are you coming with us to *messa di mezzanotte*? Please do." A small boy asked the question. Midnight mass. It seemed the right thing. It would be interesting. Besides, how could they refuse the pleading in his black eyes?

"I bet he gets his own way all the time," Judy whispered.

Outside the church a Christmas tree – the first they'd seen – towered like an altar. Inside, old ladies in black held tight to the hands of fidgety children as the priest chanted, the congregation echoing his words. At midnight exactly, a procession shuffled its way along marbled aisles, between columns, beneath chandeliers that reflected the light from hundreds of candles. The Christ child was placed in a life size crib; the choir sang joyously whilst Judy sneezed, her nose irritated by the clouds of incense.

Afterwards there were fireworks, dazzling sparks of colour splashed across the black sky. Trailing home behind *La Signora,* her small and neatly moustached husband, various friends and neighbours carrying sleeping children like sacks over their shoulders, Judy spotted what she thought was a firefly.

"I doubt it. Too cold." Pete sighed at her disappointed face. "But then again, who knows? Anything is possible in this place."

"Exactly."

Early the next morning she was sick. Hunger, she decided, and ate half of Pete's bread as well as her own.

"Hey, love. You know how I feel about fat women!"

It was a joke between them, Judy a feminist. Believing women have a right to be any shape they choose. Just the same, she stayed slim. She didn't try, never dieted, it was against her beliefs. She just never seemed to gain weight.

"I'll walk off the calories up in the mountains."

They'd planned to spend the day away from the house, not wanting to intrude on the family. They didn't get past the front door.

It was the children who caught at their knees, pulling them into the kitchen where the long table seemed to sag beneath plates, glasses, bottles. The tablecloth was stiff as paper.

"No, but really. We..."

"*Si, si.*" Take a seat. What will you have to drink?"

The husband had already been drinking. Usually silent, now he chatted, continually on the move, welcoming new arrivals with a jovial slap, with kisses full on the lips of those women not quick enough to turn laughingly aside. Most of them were. Most of them knew him well.

La Signora, when she emerged, was stunning in red silk, high heels to match. She smiled a little, even laughed when someone remarked how young she was looking. Had she taken a lover, he added; she blushed the colour of her dress.

The kitchen was packed. Some people spoke a little English, one in particular, a girl who had spent three months in London. She translated for them when necessary, delighted when they understood.

They felt at ease with the family, not strangers and yet not special guests either. People simply accepted them. Yet though they felt relaxed, and privileged, and increasingly merry, still they were drawn together by that feeling of being out of context. Of being part of a group and yet not belonging.

Later, after a meal of spaghetti and fish and broccoli dark as the cypress trees that could be seen up behind the house, the trees that circled the cemetery where so many of the family were now at rest, but remembered still as tears filled faded eyes, Christmas being a time for remembering; later, Pete's secret was revealed. It was the children who gave him away. *E uno buffone*. Piling him up with apples, scraping aside tables and chairs, they insisted. He had no choice but to give in. Shy at first, he felt foolish juggling fruit, then grew more confident as even the adults were impressed. There were encores. He felt good, as though he'd contributed something to the day, hadn't come completely empty-handed.

And later still the singing began, and the dancing. And then the drunken disagreements, the apologies, the tears. The splendid reconciliation that was an excuse for everyone to fill their glasses yet again. Just like last Christmas, someone said. And the one before, someone else added. Glasses were raised.

Curled up against Pete's shoulder, comfortable, tired but unable to sleep, Judy thought again of her own family. Of the kind of day they would have had: quiet, pleasant, less flamboyant than the one she had just spent. But a happy day. She hoped so anyway.

They escaped to the mountains next day, on foot, stopping often to look at the breath-taking views, a wildflower, a mountain spring converted into a fountain at which travellers were invited to drink, to be refreshed. A hunter passed them, gun under his arm, a bunch of birds, quail, woodcock, tied and slung like a scarf around his neck. He glanced at them, unused to seeing strangers on the steep narrow track. It saddened Judy, the small soft corpses, a few drops of blood trailing from a fresher wound, speckling the ground. Blood. It reminded her. Could she really be pregnant? It was possible. But it was also possible that it was a false alarm. Not surprisingly her whole system was disorientated these days.

Still, she should say something to Pete, shouldn't she? Like, warn him? It wasn't just that, of course. She needed to share her thoughts, her worries, that ridiculous twinge of joy she was feeling with someone. Not just someone. With Pete.

"Let's sit here a minute," he said, pulling her towards a low wall covered with moss. They balanced side by side.

"I want to talk to you, Jude. It's just... well, I've been thinking..."

"Me too," She couldn't wait. "I want to talk, I mean."

"OK. You first."

She told him.

His face was like the sea spread below them, wind rippling the surface, twisting it now this way, now that. She was relieved. So he felt exactly like she did: unsure of what he felt.

"But love, how? I don't understand. You've been taking the pill. Surely..."

"I ran out weeks ago. I don't know, it seemed so complicated to get more. And we've been so worried about money too."

She didn't look at him, it sounded so feeble. As though she were making excuses, had wanted to get pregnant. That was what bothered her most, not being sure of her own intentions.

A rabbit appeared from the undergrowth, paused, went on its way without panic. They were both so still, so lost inside themselves, it hadn't sensed their presence. Pete reached out, grasped her shoulders, turned her to face him.

"OK, Judy. I'll say it again. I love you."

She waited for him to continue.

"Big time. So much so that I'll do whatever you say. You don't fancy marriage? OK, we'll live together. No problem. If you change your mind of course, I'm more than happy to give marriage a go. After all, we've survived this trip, marriage should be a doddle."

He grinned, ran his hand through his hair.

"And if there is a baby on the way, well, that's fine too. If he has your laugh and my juggling skills, hey..."

For some reason Judy found herself blinking back tears.

Pete stood, rubbed his hands furiously, stamped his feet. It was getting cold, the sun already slipping behind the purple mountains that still seemed to tower above them. Judy stood looking out to sea.

"I don't know what I want, Pete. Apart from the fact that I don't want to ever, ever lose you."

They linked hands. Gravel scattered beneath their feet; below them the lights of the village were coming on. They thought of the bar, smoky, noisy, welcoming. Of steaming hot drinks.

"Oh and one other thing." Judy said.

"I'd like to go home. To Boston. Soon. I mean, like in the next week? I've loved the trip, it's been one of the most wonderful experiences of my life. I especially love it here in Positano. But for me, it's come to an end. I'm ready to get back to real life. Can we?"

It was later that evening when they were finally alone that she thought to ask him what it was he'd intended to say, up there in the hills.

"Oh that. I was just going to say, let's go home, shall we?"

"See how in tune we are?" She grinned as he pulled her close.

AT THE BAR

You don't expect things to change. You want them not to. You want to go back year after year to the exact same paradise you first fell in love with, where everything is exactly as it was the day you arrived.

Like the bar.

It was always open, it seemed, even on those pearl pale mornings when you got up at six to go on a trip to Capri or Rome and gathered in a small still group on the corner outside the bar, no-one about, waiting patiently for the coach that was inevitably late, the driver hung over and bad tempered after a night spent celebrating his cousin's feast day. Then the bar was already open, Federico inside, sweeping, organising chairs, a fat man dressed in the same brown as the doughnuts he was arranging neatly in trays, the *cornetti*, the *babas*, all still warm from the baker's oven.

Or when you'd been out for an evening meal, then a walk along the beach to watch the two moons, one overhead, the other bobbing about in the inky sea like a tennis ball, and suddenly found you were weary, but not ready to give up and retire to bed, not yet. Then Federico was still there, still working.

He always looked tired, shadows under his eyes, shoulders sloping, feet shuffling across the tiled floor as though too heavy to pick up. His skin was pale as lard.

"How not?" he would ask, splaying fat fingers. "I am always here, I never stop working. You know when I last had a holiday? Me, no. I don't remember."

And he would grin in a way that said, but it's alright, I wouldn't have it any other way. He loved his work, meeting people, showing off the smattering of languages he knew, a little English, French, German. *Spa seeba, da sveedanya.* Thank you, goodbye in Russian. *Vaer sa god,* you're welcome in Norwegian. Or was it Swedish? Not that many Russians or Norwegians came to the village. Or that he'd know them if they did, despite the pride he took in his ability to guess people's nationalities.

Sometimes he was right. Blondes he usually spoke to in German, especially if they were wearing yellow. Americans were easy: it was their gloss, their polish that gave them away. Also the name tags they wore as though they themselves needed reassurance as to who they were, where they were from, disorientated by breakfasting in one country, sleeping in another. According to Federico, anyone who was obviously homosexual was Dutch, only the Dutch were so open about it, held hands, kissed in public.

He liked the English best.

"*Sono simpatici,*" he would explain. Many of them were. Nice young newlyweds in shorts, with the glow that comes from nights of togetherness. Elderly couples toting string bags full of gifts: ceramic pipe holders, miniature bottles of Strega, souvenirs for sons and grandsons in Stoke Newington and Norwich. Lace places mats for daughters-in-law to put in drawers and forget.

Others were homesick. Or drank too much, Or - just now and again - complained loud enough to be heard over the shushing of the Gaggia, about the people at a nearby table, so common with their handkerchief hats and sunburnt backs, typical tourists. Or about the fan not working properly, or the weakness of the tea, hardly worth drinking, lukewarm too. Or being served cakes on paper napkins.

"You'd think he could put it on a plate!"

"Trying to save himself work. They're bone lazy, these people."

Federico would smile, move away, not understanding. Or choosing not to. His attitude to life was a positive one: he saw good in most everyone, and if he didn't he looked away. He believed in being happy.

"Soon enough I am up there," he would say, pointing way up above the houses to the little cemetery with its ring of black cypresses. "Today, I laugh. I smile. I live."

His customers agreed.

The word was passed around. "Go to Fred's. He'll see you alright."

And because of him the bar had an atmosphere, something undefinable yet as tangible as the stainless-steel counter Federico was forever wiping, polishing, till you could see yourself in it. Above hung seven lampshades lighting up the display cabinets with their pastel ice creams, shiny fruit flans, mozzarella *panin*i. With boxes of English chocolates, a taste of home, though if you bought them you'd probably find they were stale and stuck together by heat and time.

On the walls were pictures of film stars of the fifties: Marilyn Monroe, Doris Day, Gina Lollobrigida, faded portraits of stars who'd long ago lost their glitter. Except for Federico.

"My harem." He would roll his eyes, blow them kisses.

He had a soft spot for all the ladies, gave them flowers from the copper jug that stood at the end of the counter, roses, geraniums, gladioli, whatever was in season. He'd walk away before anyone could thank him.

Federico, the romantic.

It was more than a bar. More like a club. People left messages with Federico, scribbling on backs of envelopes, calling across from the doorway. He remembered them all, though sometimes a little late so that he had to run out into the street after someone, breathless, squinting in the dazzling sunlight. Suitcases were left, parcels. A white poodle who was being passed from owner to friend and who spent a whole afternoon coyly begging titbits, peed up a table leg, then threw up.

Locals handed in their *totocalcio* forms, crossed and kissed for luck. Few people in the village won, and then never much, a few million lire. But with football pools it's always possible. Men in tattered trousers, unshaven, bought drinks they couldn't afford on a wave of optimism. Often Federico forgot to charge them.

And then.

Then there were the children, of course, packs of them hanging from his arms like monkeys from a tree, giggling, dodging as he tried to flap them away. Knowing that in the end he'd give in and give them sweets, *amaretti*, raising his eyebrows in mock exasperation.

Federico adored children. Anyone could see that.

"Is he married?" people asked, visitors here for the first time and instantly at ease with this fat, smiling man. Wanting him to have a wife, a family, a house somewhere along the coast road where he would be the pampered one, would sit out under a sky soft and black as the caged blackbird that would chirp amusement as he told tales of his day at the bar.

No-one seemed to know though there were plenty of rumours. He'd once been married to a real beauty who'd died in childbirth. Or had gone off with a man who worked for a computer company in Milan. Or shot herself, or become a nun. Or she was very plain, he'd married her out of pity.

"A wife? Why I need a wife?" was his usual reply, running his hand across hair that was beginning to thin on top, you could just see his skin through it when he bent to put down your cappuccino. No-one knew his age either. He could have been in his thirties, forties. Sometimes it was hard to believe he was under fifty.

Three or four times during the season he would say it was his birthday, would offer free drinks, pour one for himself, get out his mandolin and start a singsong that went on into the early hours. Locals shrugged and joined in, none of them mentioning the fact that he'd had just such a celebration a few months ago. So if there was no reason to have a party, he'd invent one. What was wrong with that? He was eccentric yes. A little bit *pazzo*. But you couldn't help but like him.

And so the years passed, and nothing much changed.

Tourists came, a trickle early in the year, a flood in August, then the numbers tailed off.

The locals were always in and out of the place, everyone from the fishermen to the mayor.

The village priest called in most days, often turning to Federico for his opinion on some matter or other, enjoying the small whisky that was put down in front of him, no charge of course. Federico thought it wise to keep in with God, just in case.

Mid mornings the tourists came in for their *cappuccinos,* often having more than one, were still spooning the creamy froth from the top when school closed and the school bus spilled scores of blue-smocked children into the bar where they skidded about like marbles, were quickly retrieved by their mothers.

In the afternoons – in the lull – Federico would flop into a corner seat and dig into a bag of crisps as he flicked through a comic, or put on the TV that hung high on the wall and watched some silly game, or even the news.

Then late afternoons the crowds would head back from the beach, hot and thirsty, stopping off for a drink before returning to their hotels to freshen up for the evening, would relax inside under the listless fan sipping long pink drinks, or outside on the pavement, feet virtually in the road, knees grazed by passing cars, loving it all.

The routine never changed, and neither did Federico. He was exactly what people expected him to be: always welcoming, always there.

When he disappeared, it was a shock.

The ripples spread to far-flung northern cities where they caused consternation amongst those who summered each year in the village by the sea. No-one could believe it. The bar itself looked exactly the same, was run now by a cousin who looked very much like Federico. Only he wasn't anything at all like him, he was business-like, aloof. He didn't chat. He rarely laughed.

"But where is Federico?" everyone asked. Had he – he hadn't surely – had he died?

The village shut up like a clam. There were abrupt changes of subject, uncomfortable silences. Someone even said "Federico who?" It was as though he'd never existed. And then, in a car parked by the beach one midnight, dazzled by the proximity of a pink and perfumed northern girl, a nephew of Federico's was persuaded to talk.

Federico had been caught tampering with children. It had happened more than once. He had admitted it. He was sick in the head. He was disgusting, added the nephew, with the typical Italian protectiveness towards children, as he nibbled her dainty ear and shuffled closer. She pulled back. And where was he now, Federico?

He'd been sent away; the villagers had insisted. Over the other side of the mountains to live with elderly relatives where there were no innocents he could molest, no harm he could do. Far, far away from people.

He was a disgrace to the family name.

The story got around with the speed of the scooters that zipped noisily along the narrow streets. Though the details remained much the same, the emphasis shifted.

Federico was considered to be not so much a villain as a victim.

"If only he'd had a wife, children of his own…"

"They worked him too hard. He was supporting a whole family, you know. Mother, brothers and sisters. Something has to crack under that kind of strain."

"Load of rubbish. Must be more to it than they're saying. Federico would never behave like that. I've known him for ten years, more, and he was always the perfect gentleman."

"Poor man. He'll go crazy on his own. Never known anyone who enjoyed the company of other people as much as he did."

The bar no longer drew the crowds. People actually avoided it, crossed the street, and found a new favourite. Doris Day slipped down behind the counter that now stocked packets of biscuits, tinned nuts, nothing fresh. Dead flies collected in corners. The fan stopped working and wasn't repaired. The bar opened late and closed early.

One day it closed down completely.

A businessman from Rome had bought the property. He stocked it with ashtrays, toys, sunhats made in Macau, sandals from Thailand.

For a while Federico's bar was still talked about by visitors. Gradually people mentioned it less often. Then those who'd frequented it lost their taste for the village altogether, for southern Italy; grew richer and went on tours of Australia and the Far East, or bought time shares in villas in Key West. Without them to keep the legend alive, it faded away completely.

Up in the mountains Federico lived on pasta and grew fatter than ever.

EARTHQUAKES AND MINOR SHOCKS

When Howard switched off the car engine silence settled around them like dust. The dust itself took a little longer, but eventually the cloud cleared and they could see what they had come to see: a village in ruins.

"Oh, but just imagine, Howard. It must have been beautiful. And the views. We're so high we could almost be flying."

Anna was high on just being there. At long last. They clambered out of the car, flexed muscles that were sore after the long ride up into the mountains. They'd left their hotel after an early breakfast. They'd got lost three times; had taken two hours longer than Howard had anticipated, and he rarely misjudged, was famed for his ability to get you from A to B in the quickest time. That's without breaking the speed limit, of course.

Still, this was southern Italy, not Surrey. He'd done his best.

As he was bent fiddling with the keys, unfamiliar with the hired car, a tornado struck, a small black dog from out of nowhere, snarling and snapping like a crazy thing, a dust storm with teeth. Anna screamed. Howard kicked at it but missed. Then, abruptly, the dog spun around and was gone.

"Phew." Anna's face wore bright pink patches. She checked the hem of her white trousers for dirt, teeth marks, unable to believe that she hadn't been touched; re-adjusted her straw hat to the rakish angle on which she'd decided after ten minutes in front of the mirror. Howard took off his steel-rimmed glasses, rubbed them, put them back on again.

"Vicious brute. Probably has rabies. It's common here, you know. Even the bats carry it."

"Thank you, Howard. What a comfort you are."

Anna worried about germs, diseases; even chipped cups made her shudder. She carried a tube of antiseptic cream with her wherever she went. The thought of being bitten by a dog was bad enough, but a rabid dog, that was the stuff of nightmares.

But no, nothing was going to spoil this day. The sky was cloudless and that travel brochure blue that usually accompanies a stretch of deserted beach. Here the sea was far away, yet surrounded as they were by greenery, by shrubs, trees, tiers of vineyards, they could have been on an island; an isolated white farmhouse could have been a distant sailing boat.

Still Anna couldn't believe it. She was here at last, in the village where her father had been born the ninth of thirteen children, had grown into a lanky teenager, telling for years tales of that childhood: of the fractious goat who ate the priest's cassock, was forgiven and blessed and never the same again. Of barefooted walks where snakes slithered quick as spaghetti, but still got trodden on, causing cries and consternation. Of stealing peaches as sweet and fat as Lucia, the girl he'd been in love with when they were both ten, who'd never married but had nursed an ailing sister until, when she died, Lucia had no reason to carry on living. She'd hung herself from an olive tree.

He told that story often, it was a favourite. God rest her soul, he would add, though he wasn't much of a churchgoer. On summer Sundays he preferred picnics in the moist green countryside, was never bothered about bulls or ants or wasps' nests. Anna, like her mother, had endured the outings, sitting neatly, warily on a rug and wishing she were elsewhere, somewhere safe, with walls.

He'd never wanted to return to the village, her father. As though in a photograph album, he had his memories tucked tidily away, could flick through them whenever he wanted. But like photos they belonged to the past. In later years he drank tea, wore a bowler hat, loved Yorkshire pudding, though he still sang opera to himself. *Pagliacci* was a favourite. It was so wonderfully sad.

It wasn't until he died that Anna felt the need to see where he'd come from, to find his roots. Hers too of course. Seeking one's roots was a very 'in' thing to do.

But she should have come sooner.

Now she stood with her husband in the empty square and everything shimmered. It was hot, almost unbearably so. Amongst the ruins poppies were scattered like drops of blood where real blood had been spilled only a few years ago as houses came crashing down on the sleeping villagers, crushing them, burying them beneath bricks and rubble that would take rescuers days, weeks to clear.

Anna knew all the details. She'd been glued to the television. The earthquake had struck at 4.20am on a January night when there was snow on the ground. People a hundred miles away had been woken by cups tinkling in cabinets. Many had died, over 90 in this village alone, 12 on this very spot. An epitaph listed the names of those who had run to the church for safety, had managed to get inside just before it crumbled like a sandcastle. The epitaph had been placed where the altar once stood. Anna's family name did not appear.

"Come on, darling. Let's look around."

They climbed a narrow, twisting road between houses that were still intact, old houses, tall and sombre, with wrought iron balconies hung over twists of steps that led up to heavy wooden doors. One of them opened a crack, shut quietly after they'd passed.

A tabby cat lay curled in a pool of sunlight, tail twitching. Anna skirted it. She thought of asking Howard if cats too could carry rabies but decided against. Better not to know.

An old lady in black, her broad face arranged in folds, made her way slowly down the hill, a basket balanced on her head, hand touching the wall to steady her. Her unblinking eyes were black with suspicion. Still Howard nodded, Anna smiled warmly; wished she could say something that would prove they were not strangers, but that they had a right to be there. That in a way they belonged. But she didn't speak Italian well; her father hadn't used it at home, not even with the other members of his family who had followed him to London in twos and threes until they were all together again, the pull of family strong as a magnet. She tried, though. At the hotel they understood almost everything she said, and in the market she'd haggled over the price of a leather bag, and won. Later she would get out her dictionary and have a go.

At the top of the hill the road faded away, the houses stopped. Turning back on themselves they cut down dark passages, steps, found themselves in a completely different part of the village. Though the houses were of a more modern style, white and square as sugar cubes, the damage here was far worse. Rooftops were missing, doors and windows gone so that only facades were left. Other houses, some inhabited – there were geraniums growing in coffee tins, singing coming from an open window – were undamaged except for cracks like zigzags of lightning down outside walls. From a first-floor balcony chickens peered and muttered, then set up a flutter as a man came from inside, put down food, stood gazing along the street and scratching his head.

Now there were occasional shops, too: a grocers, a *tabaccaio*, another with carcasses, red and raw, smelling of decay and spotted with flies.

"Did you see inside? That could put you off meat for life, couldn't it?" said Anna, thinking of the neat pink packs she bought at the supermarket.

They found a bar.

"At last. I knew there had to be one somewhere."

"It's a bit early to start drinking, don't you…?"

Howard ignored her, pushed aside the beaded curtain. It was more like someone's living room than a bar, except for the calendar depicting a blonde wearing only suspender belt and stockings; it was three years out of date. On all the tables were empty glasses, full ashtrays. Using just fingertips, Anna cleared a space on one. They sat.

A man ambled over to serve them drying his hands on a rag. He was balding, just a little at the front, his plaid shirt pulled tight over a paunch. Anna asked for wine. He shook his head.

"*Non c'e vino.*"

"No wine? Really? Alright. *Due Campari sodas con ghiaccio, per favore.*"

There was no ice either. Anna and Howard exchanged glances. Their drinks tasted warm and flat. Two men came into the bar, barefooted, filling the small room with their loud voices, their laughter that Anna felt was directed at her and Howard, the way they kept glancing across, though she couldn't understand their dialect at all. It was another language.

"Go on." Howard nudged her arm. "Ask."

She felt suddenly nervous.

"You won't find if you've got any relatives if you don't ask."

"It's easy for you to say."

He was right, of course. Anna took the plunge, repeated her question twice before understanding flickered across the barman's face. He shrugged thick shoulders, turned to the two men who had been listening with him. They discussed the matter, or at least, they seemed to be genuinely doing so. Names were thrown back and forth. Then one of the men came up with something.

"*Si?*" The barman's eyes opened a fraction wider. He looked at Anna long and hard. Telling her to wait, he disappeared through a door, his footsteps heavy as he went upstairs and into a room directly overhead.

The two men drained their glasses, nodded goodbye. The bar seemed emptier than ever, the buzz of a trapped fly loud as a drill. Howard polished his glasses. Anna dabbed cologne on her throat, her wrists.

The barman returned with an elderly man, thin and bent, his baggy trousers so long they touched the floor. His eyes, though, sparkled. He walked up to Anna, hesitated, then reached out and gripped her shoulders with curved, bony hands.

"So you are Luigi's daughter?" She sensed rather than understood his meaning.

"Yes, I see it. You may be pale and skinny like an English woman, but those eyes, they are Italian. So dark, such melancholy."

He laughed showing brown teeth; he smelled of cigarettes and needed a shave. He pinched her cheek.

"But you don't know who I am? Of course not. I am Paolo, a cousin of your father's. Ah but we had some good times together when we were boys. I remember, even now, after all these years."

He bent close.

"You must call me papa. Everyone does."

He introduced the barman as Sergio, his son. Anna introduced Howard. Hands were shaken. Anna felt confused, happy that she'd found a relative – what would he be? An uncle? A second cousin? – but aware that he didn't feel like someone she was related to. He felt like a stranger. Worse still, she wasn't sure that she liked him much. Nor his scruffy, morose son.

They sat, more drinks were poured.

"Now, tell me about everyone." Papa was all attention. Anna concentrated. Together they picked up the threads of people's lives, followed them until they reached a point where they tangled with familiar names, events.

"You must know Gianni. No? He's the son of Rosa. Or was Franca his mother? *Si, e vero.* Rosa."

Too often they were dead. Anna felt somehow responsible. Wasn't it the ancient Romans who used to kill the messenger bearing bad news?

"Alfonso? *Mi dispiace ma...*" She turned to Howard as though to bring him into the conversation to share the guilt. "How do you say heart attack?" Howard looked blank. Papa sighed, crossed himself yet again.

Sergio refilled their glasses, Anna's stomach rumbled. She needed to find a toilet, too, would have to ask. She dreaded to think what state it would be in.

The doorway darkened as a large woman in a flowered dress entered, a tight white knot on her head, a child attached to each hand. A younger woman followed, neat and silent as a shadow. There was something almost regal about the older woman; everyone stood.

"*Ecco*, my wife." Papa introduced her proudly. "My daughter-in-law. And my two beautiful *nipoti*." He snatched playfully at his grandchildren as they swarmed around his legs, nearly knocked him flying.

"*Dov'e Nero?*" Mama, frowning now, crossed to the beaded curtain, swished it aside. "*Nero, vieni qui tesoro!*"

She bent to scoop up the small black dog that came running, hugged and kissed him. A familiar dog, though now it looked older, tattier, seemed to be blind in one eye.

"He is fourteen. You understand?" Mama traced the numerals in the air with Pentel-like fingers. One. Four. "You like dogs?"

Anna and Howard nodded, Howard even managed to bring himself to pat the hot, matted head. Anna thought how it should be put down, it was cruel to keep it alive. It smelt awful.

"And now we eat."

Anna's protestations were ignored. Howard said why not? Tables were pushed together, a cloth found. From the kitchen upstairs soon came the smells of onions, peppers, the chattering of the two women. One of the children was screamed at, slapped, burst into tears and started the dog barking.

Wine was produced.

"*Vino di casa*. Our own. We don't sell it in the bar. There is no profit..."

Sergio filled their glasses, over generous in his embarrassment. Anna forgave him. She was beginning to feel much warmer to them all, her family. In the toilet she had a sudden fit of the giggles.

Food appeared now, great platters of spaghetti, cheese to sprinkle on top, bread the colour and texture of porridge. Sergio tore chunks off the loaf with his hands, passed them around, and Anna didn't mind that either. Everyone wiped their plates clean with bread and more food arrived, slices of dark meat, a green vegetable that looked like spinach, but wasn't. Anna and Howard gave up on conversation. Their hosts, however, became more talkative, told tales of the village, local people, not unlike those Anna's father used to tell, though the one they returned to again and again was the earthquake in all its details. A drama to beat all dramas.

"But we're lucky to be here, we survivors. So many good friends..."

There was a sombre moment, Anna and Howard feeling the awkwardness that comes with being an outsider. A choking sound: the dog was being sick. The children giggled with delight, the daughter-in-law tight lipped as she went for rags, water. Mama was concerned. Amidst the chaos Anna was just in time to notice Howard lean forward, touch his head to the table, and fall asleep.

"Howard," she whispered, kicking at his ankle.

"What? What is it?" He started, yawned, removed his glasses. "Need a coffee, that will wake me up. Early start, a lot of driving, it's no wonder I can't keep my eyes open."

He smiled at Anna, not quite focussing.

Through the open door they could see the light was already changing to amber, softening as the sun slid down in the sky. A few cars passed, people peered in, called *ciao*. A van delivered cartons of beer. The day was going; Anna had wanted to walk around some more, visit the cemetery. There wouldn't be time. It felt like they'd been eating for hours.

Coffee came, strong and black and served in tiny cups. And then, because it was a celebration, *una festa* – they'd put a notice saying as much on the door so they wouldn't be disturbed – a special liqueur was brought out from a cupboard, dark purple, a taste of blackberries, sweet and sharp at the same time. Mama had made it herself, it was her speciality.

They had a glass, said how delicious, were pressed to have another. And a third. It really was delicious.

And suddenly the world outside was black, their hotel room a long way away. And they both felt so exhausted they could hardly keep their eyes open.

"You must stay the night." That was Papa.

"No, no. We must get back to the hotel. Another coffee and then…"

"You stay. You are our guests." Mama this time. She sounded reluctant but resigned.

No point in trying to refuse, in insisting they didn't want to put anyone out. They realised that. Mama led them up the steep dark stairway to the small flat in which the whole family seemed to live, along a corridor to a room crowded with heavy, highly polished furniture. A picture of Christ on the cross hung over the bed. It was obviously Sergio and his wife's room and Anna felt dreadful about turning them out and making them sleep – where? On the floor? Still, what could she do?

It was an effort to strip down to their underwear, but they managed, fell into bed at once. And now, suddenly, they were wide awake. The bed dipped and had lumps. The room was hot and airless, and when they managed to open a window they were invaded by mosquitoes; Howard complained he was being bitten to death. Eventually they put on the light and, as quietly as possible, smashed those they were quick enough to catch against the white walls where they left blood stains.

"My blood," moaned Howard.

"My stomach!"

Anna realised she needed the bathroom. Urgently.

On the way back a figure emerged from one of the rooms leading off the corridor, caught her arm. It was Papa.

"Shh," He held one finger against her lips. Then he tried to kiss her. She was too tired to be angry. It was all too silly. And it wouldn't hurt her, he was a nice enough old man. Just one kiss. Besides, he was becoming more insistent. He'd waken everyone, there would be a scene. It would be awful. She gave in, gave him her lips. His were coarse and dry as sandpaper. And then she felt his fingers working their way up under her bra. She pulled away.

"No," she whispered loudly, insistently. "That's enough."

Howard asked who she'd been talking to in the corridor. She said the dog.

When eventually she fell asleep she dreamed of earthquakes, of walls trembling around her, the ground cracking like an egg shell and she was falling down into blackness. Why do I never dream of nice things? she thought, forcing herself awake. Howard was snoring gently. It was a familiar, comforting sound.

In the morning his face and neck were covered in bites swollen up big as boils. He was scratching furiously.

"Do stop it. You'll start up an infection," said Anna.

Everyone else was already up, though on seeing them the daughter-in-law claimed to have a headache, and retired to bed. The children, uncontrolled now, set about destroying the place. Papa gazed at Anna with moist, hurt eyes, unnoticed by Mama who was too busy fussing the dog which, she insisted, was sickening for something.

Sergio blamed Howard's bites on his fair skin, managing to make it sound like a weakness.

Anna wouldn't have admitted it but she was relieved to be leaving. She indulged in thoughts of their crisp, cool hotel room, a shower, a drink in the bar with its creaking leather sofas and polished tile floor. And ice in their drinks, lots of it, nicely crushed. The way these people lived, well, it was almost primitive.

"It was wonderful to meet you all. Thanks again for everything. *Per tutto.*"

Everyone kissed them both on both cheeks, Howard shy with the men, Anna ready for Papa to take advantage of the situation, to grope her under the guise of a fatherly hug. Which he did. The children refused to be kissed, threw tantrums when Sergio insisted.

Anna and Howard walked back to the car, relieved to find it still there, wound down the windows to let out air that was already stifling. They promised they would drive past the bar – one last goodbye – somehow found their way back through the maze of streets. The family was waiting, lined up on the pavement, waving. Anna waved back, Howard pressed the horn.

Suddenly Nero raced from inside the bar barking, jumping up and down at the doors of the car, trying to bite the wheels. Howard slowed down. There was the smallest bump, then silence.

"My God, I think you've hit him." Anna squirmed in her seat, looking back, trying to see. Mama was racing across the road. Howard braked.

By the time they'd reluctantly got out of the car and reached the dog it was surrounded by a circle of legs, Mama in the centre cradling the still body in her huge arms, her face crumpled.

"Is he alright?" Howard was furious for asking the question, could have kicked himself, though it didn't matter, no-one understood. The dog was obviously dead.

On seeing them Mama started to scream.

Murderers, she screamed, traitors who had come pretending to be of the same blood, the same family. Had eaten their food, taken their beds. And given what in return? This, she cried, lifting up the dog's limp body. This.

Anna didn't need to translate. Both Howard and she backed away. Sergio stepped up to them, pulled them aside.

"Better go. Don't worry, she'll get over it. The dog was old anyway."

He pushed them gently in the direction of the car.

Other people were joining the group, passers-by. Expressions were serious.

Howard wiped his forehead, his glasses. As they drove off this time no-one waved or even noticed, only one small boy who brandished a tight fist and called something they couldn't hear. Anna sighed, settled back in her seat. They were lucky to have got away at all.

"Italians!" she said. "I don't think I'll ever really understand them."

She pulled Howard's hand away from the bite he was attacking on his neck and wondered if they would be back in time for a swim in the hotel pool.

LIMONCELLO

"Mister Danny? *Per favore*, open the door. I know you are there."

No way, Daniel muttered, hunkered down behind the tatty brown leather sofa, knees burning on the brittle tiles, aware that his left leg was about to cramp. He was too old to be hiding behind sofas. He was too bulky. He was way too hot, couldn't believe how hot it was considering it was only April. He wiped his forehead with the back of his wrist.

And what was his neighbour doing knocking on his door so early anyway? They had an unspoken agreement: never crowd each other, never intrude. He must have seen his lights come on last night, even though Daniel had arrived much later than planned – the middle of the night really - the gruff Neapolitan taxi driver dumping him at the top of the village, anxious to get home to his wife no doubt, leaving Daniel to stumble his way down the badly lit steps. His suitcase had weighed a ton, he'd had to keep putting it down: a cat - intent on torturing some small creature - suddenly shot past, stopping only to hiss at him.

Yeah, you too buddy, he thought.

He'd sat outside on the doorstep for a while to get his bearings before plucking up courage to open the door and go inside. He'd forgotten how wonderfully black the sky was here away from the city, how the stars were so sharp they hurt your eyes.

"OK, Mister Danny. I go. *Ti lascio qualcosa*."

Footsteps crunching on gravel. The clang of a heavy iron gate. Then, silence. Daniel got cautiously to his feet, massaged his leg. He limped to the front door, knowing what he'd find even before he opened it. On the doorstep, a small white cardboard box. He could feel the warmth as he picked it up. Inside would be two *cornetti*, golden and flaky and fresh from the oven. He knew what the filling would be too: Nutella. Kurt's favourite.

"Shit."

In an instant he'd crossed the kitchen and dropped the box into the bin, blinking back tears as he was doused in a shower of memories.

Kurt and him on the way back from someone's god child's feast day celebrations up in the mountains above Montepertuso, way past midnight, passing the tiny shop that didn't need a sign to say it was a bakery.

"Wow, that smell…"

"Hungry?"

"Famished. But are they open?"

"They're baking for tomorrow morning," Daniel had said. "But they won't mind us going in."

"Lead on."

Inside the small room people in white aprons bustling, singing along to the music from an unseen radio. Everywhere, trays of golden delights. Even the air was a golden haze. They'd emerged with pastries so hot they'd had to keep passing them from hand to hand.

Or, a morning when they'd gone early to the beach, stopped off for *cornetti* and coffee, standing at the bar alongside fishermen back from a night's work, the girl with yellow hair who sold tickets for boat trips to Capri, the priest, powdered sugar down the front of his cassock. Being edged aside as more locals arrived, calling their order as they came through the door, impatient to get their day started, but always smiling.

"It's not just another country," Kurt had said. "It's another mind set.".

Or back in New York, recipe book propped against a kettle, Kurt's hands covered in flour as he tried yet again to make a decent *cornetto*. It was a commitment, all that kneading, sitting and waiting whilst the dough slowly rose, more kneading, more waiting, cutting, filling, folding. It seemed to take days.

"Why bother?" Daniel had said. "We know where to get them. When the craving gets too much, we can just hop on a flight."

"You can. You're a successful ad man. I'm a struggling lyricist."

"And actor, a good one." He was branching out and doing surprisingly well. With a bit of help from Daniel, which he hated of course.

"Lyricist, actor, whatever. I still can't afford a flight to Boston let alone Naples."

One of the things they'd argued about. Kurt didn't want Daniel to pay for him all the time, Daniel didn't want to live a frugal life, not now he didn't need to any more. He planned to be indulgent, reckless, to make the most of every day. He'd been renting the house in Positano for ten years; finally, finally he could afford to enjoy it.

"I want to munch my *cornetti* gazing at the ocean," he'd said. "Not Riverside Drive."

"So look at the river and pretend," Kurt had replied, carefully rolling up the flattened dough triangles, bringing in the sides to make a crescent shape.

"There. How do you say it in Italian? *Perfetto*?"

They disagreed about so many things, were forever fighting. Opposites attract, their friends said when one of them – usually

Kurt – stormed out leaving the other one to shrug, make light of it all, carry on as though everything was alright. Was it true? Danny wondered. Their life together was full of friction, sulks, breaking up and making up, like the Hollywood romantic comedies that made millions at the box office. But real life wasn't a movie. He wasn't Bruce Willis or Tom Cruise. Sometimes he found it all a bit tedious, a waste of energy. But then, when he tried to imagine life without Kurt, there was just a gaping hole.

He'd been right. Living without Kurt was somehow... pointless.

Outside there was the sudden clatter of children running down the steps, a shout and then laughter. Playing truant. Good for you, kids, Daniel thought.

And now the smell of the pastries was getting to him. It was understandable, he hadn't eaten since his meal on the flight over, and he'd left most of that. The large woman squeezed into the seat next to him had chain smoked her way across the Atlantic. Sorry, she'd said. My nerves. After a bit he'd felt sick. His own fault, he should have insisted on a seat at the front.

Come to that, everything was his fault.

He retrieved the box from the bin. There must be some instant coffee in the cupboard, probably so stale he'd have to chip it out, but that would do. And then, to work.

No more reminiscing. No more thinking. Thinking wasn't going to get the place tidied up, things boxed to go back to the US, everything ready for when Guido arrived this afternoon. Guido, his landlord but also his friend. He'd be disappointed to hear Daniel was giving up the house. Shocked. He'd probably take it personally, be insulted.

"My house is not good for you anymore? You find another you like better?"

He was going to miss Guido, had always liked sparring with him. Could recall the early days when Daniel had been trying to gently persuade him to remove most of the modern pine furniture he'd filled the rooms with, obviously deciding that this is what his lodger would prefer. Eventually Daniel had given up on the tactful approach.

"Please. Leave this, this, that cupboard thing, the bed. Everything else I want gone by the time I get back from New York. *Hai capito? Tutto?*"

Now he looked around the room; at the chinoiserie curtains with their red elephant design, the velvet covered dining chairs tucked under the dark wood table he'd got for a song at a backstreet market in Salerno – he was sure it was 18th century rosewood but hadn't let on. Nothing but a candelabra could have gone on it. The paintings, many of them given to him by the artist. Or sold to him if times were especially hard. Everything had a story, everything belonged here in this house. How could he even start to dismantle it, it would be like taking apart his world?

But he didn't have a choice, did he?

Later then.

First thing he had to do was find the cups: Spode, with an intricate blue design inspired by the Italian countryside. He'd got them last time he was here. Perfect for serving the Earl Grey tea Guido always drank when he came to visit, said he couldn't get it anywhere else on the Amalfi coast. Probably nowhere in southern Italy. Daniel had brought some with him.

It was whilst crouched down rummaging in the back of a cupboard that he found the bottles. Seven of them, all empty now. He sniffed them, knew instantly what they'd contained. Another blow to the stomach. He sat back on his heels. Kurt and his limoncello. What was it he used to say? It smells like summer, it's the colour of happiness. Tastes like syrup, Daniel would mutter.

They clunked as he dropped them on top of the empty pastry box. One smashed.

When Guido arrived his smile was wide.

"Finally, at long last you return."

He grasped Daniel's hand between both of his, seemed reluctant to let go but then did so and stepped inside. Everything was spic and span; Daniel took pride in that. He'd pulled the shutters to keep the room cool, now placed his guest in the chenille armchair close to an open window for the air. He made tea, lowered himself onto the sofa opposite. He'd planned exactly what he was going to say.

Regretfully he had decided to terminate his contract, give in his notice, whatever the Italian expression was. To leave and not come back. Guido's eyebrows went up briefly but he didn't speak. Daniel took another deep breath.

Kurt died three months ago, he said. Three months and nineteen days to be exact. Now he was alone, and much as he loved the house and being here and the people and everything – Guido knew that, didn't he? – Daniel felt he couldn't live here anymore. Without Kurt it was just too painful. Without Kurt life was painful but he felt that if he went somewhere new where Kurt had never been, where there were no memories, no silly trinkets, nothing of Kurt, then possibly he could find a way to start over. That was the plan anyway.

Guido was a good man, he'd understand, nod, say the right things. And then of course there'd be no need for Daniel to tell anyone else because the news would spread around the village like one of the August forest fires that were always covering the mountain tops in smoke.

Now Guido sat there still holding his cup, looking at Daniel. A trapped bee bumped lazily against the closed shutter.

"It was an accident?" Guido said quietly.

"No."

"He was ill?"

"Yes. Very. Horribly."

"For a long time?"

"No. It was... I guess it was quick."

"That is good."

Daniel shrugged then nodded. No it wasn't, he wanted to say. I'd have done anything to have him with me longer, another day, another few hours, even though he was suffering, couldn't even catch his breath, was drowning in mucus, had had more than enough. I'm a selfish man, he wanted to say. Let's face it, it was all my fault he was dying.

Guido sighed, replaced the cup on its saucer. He stood. Daniel stood too. Together they walked towards the door. Then Guido turned, put his arms around Daniel shoulders, pulled him towards him and held him tightly. Neither man spoke. For the first time in months Daniel felt strangely calm.

"OK, I go," Guido said, suddenly releasing him and turning to pull open the door. Yellow light flooded the room.

"Una cosa. Devo dire non," he said, looking back at Daniel from the step. "I don't accept."

"Sorry?"

"I don't accept your resignation. This house is yours. You belong here even now, especially now."

"Guido, you don't understand..."

"Listen, we do this. You wait, you see how you feel once you are over the shock. No hurry. We talk again in a few months, maybe next year."

"But I know now what I ..."

Daniel could see here was no point in saying more. He watched as Guido walked away, stopping to pick himself a fat rose from a bush that was completely out of control, one hand raised in thanks as he reached the gate. Dead-heading the roses, that was Kurt's job, as was cutting back things that had grown too wild, sweeping leaves after a summer storm. Without Kurt, the garden would soon be a jungle.

Alone again Daniel felt suddenly exhausted, sprawled on the unmade bed. How often had they taken an afternoon nap; it's what everyone does here in the south, Daniel had said. On waking they'd reach for each other, a different kind of sex from the torrid couplings that they managed to fit into their busy schedules in New York, bodies now clammy with the heat, their movements slow and tender.

Daniel sat up again, padded into the bathroom, splashed his face with tepid water.

Could he ever tell Guido the full story? Of the day he and Kurt had had the fight about — what was it? He could hardly recall. Something trivial. He'd told Kurt to get out if that was how he felt, and Kurt had gone, caught an overnight Greyhound down to friends in Florida, stayed there for weeks until neither of them could bear to be apart any longer.

Which made it Daniel's fault, didn't it?

The gay plague, the papers called it. It seemed to arrive from nowhere.

"They think the virus came from monkeys," Kurt had said.

"You mean people have sex with monkeys?"

"Probably. But more likely it came from eating them."

"People eat monkeys?"

"Come on. You've heard of bushmeat, haven't you?"

Sometimes Daniel despaired of the human race.

That was early on when Kurt was between jobs - though he'd just done a commercial, which was how they'd met three years ago, Daniel interviewing for help with a commercial he was producing. As they liked to say – Kurt didn't get the job but he got Daniel. Now Kurt filled his time with researching this new terrifying disease that everyone was talking about. He passed on what he discovered to their friends, especially the gay ones who were worried, most of them perfectly healthy, but all knowing of someone who'd suddenly been diagnosed as positive. It felt like the virus was circling them, a hungry tiger ready to pounce. Most of them had faith that the medical profession would get it under control, and quickly. Laboratories worked twenty-four hours a day. Specialists around the world attended conferences. Money poured in. Still the number of cases soared. Deaths soared.

A side effect was that people became less tolerant of gays.

And then Daniel noticed the strange pink rash on Kurt's back. Nothing much, nothing to worry about, but maybe he should have a test, just to be sure?

Daniel of course had also taken a test. A tight-lipped female doctor had pulled on rubber gloves before – standing as far back as she could – she took hold of Daniel's arm, tapped to find a vein, syphoned off a full syringe of blood. It looked good and healthy to him. Did she disapprove? Or was she frightened? There were rumours you could catch Aids by drinking from an infected cup, kissing someone, using their toothbrush, even holding their hand.

Daniel had been lucky. He was clear. Kurt had been unlucky; he'd had sex with a stranger at a beach party under a Florida moon, just the once, he couldn't even recall the name of the guy, or how much he'd had to drink, none of it. He'd forgotten about it. It was a lifetime ago, for christ's sake.

The experts were saying not to despair, every day new drugs were coming onto the market. You could have Aids and live for months, years even.

With Kurt it progressed quickly.

All Daniel could remember of those last weeks was the feeling that he'd stepped into a parallel universe. Everything was white: the hospital walls, the pillow, the sheets, the doctor's coat that flapped as he marched in to check on Kurt, fiddled, rarely spoke, flapped out again. The only sounds were shoes squeaking on the floor, discreetly lowered voices, the click and whirr of the white machines that were keeping him alive.

Kurt's face, pale and smooth as alabaster. He was skin and bones now and Daniel thought how beautiful he was, the delicate curve of his shoulders, that fine nose.

"Promise me one thing." No more than a whisper. Daniel had had to put his ear close to Kurt's scabby lips.

"Stop blaming yourself. I got this because I was stupid, I was sulking, I wanted to punish you."

"Kurt, let's not ..."

"Promise me."

Kurt had opened his eyes, slowly and painfully turned his head towards Daniel. His dark eyes were still full of fire.

"I'll do my best."

"No. That's not enough. You have to promise."

"OK."

"Say it."

"I promise. I promise. I promise."

Three days later Kurt stopped breathing.

At his funeral there had been white roses, mounds of them on the simple coffin.

Later that evening Daniel headed out to the tiny, scruffy corner shop that proudly called itself a *supermercato*. He couldn't survive without some decent coffee, needed milk, cheese, bread. Cleaning products too. It was dusk, everything soft and mellow, streets gradually filling up with people coming out to shop, to drink aperitifs at café tables so close to the road they risked losing their toes each time a car zipped past. Daniel kept his dark glasses on, his head down, but even so a couple of locals recognized him, came over and clasped his hand, gave hesitant smiles. They knew then. He smiled back but moved on. He didn't want to talk, not yet.

Getting back to the house was a relief. He immediately put his purchases away. Kurt would have mocked. Why bother when it's just you living here? he'd have said, you can be as messy as you like. But I don't like, Daniel would have replied. Another thing they disagreed about.

A gentle knock on the door. He debated ignoring it, changed his mind.

An elderly woman, slightly hunched, grey hair pulled tightly away from her lined, worried face. What was her name? Rosa? Lucia? Damned if he could remember.

"Mister Danny. I am so, so sad."

So she knew too. Everyone did, it seemed. Daniel felt both irritated and touched. He held the door wide to invite her in but she shook her head.

"I come to give you this. Mister Kurt tells me how you both love limoncello. Here, this is my own. You understand? Not made in a factory, no rubbish ingredients. Made in my kitchen with sfusato lemons. From Amalfi, yes? The best."

She kissed her bunched fingertips to emphasis the point.

"Drink. It will make you happy."

She pressed the paper wrapped bottle into his hands and was gone.

If only it was that simple, Daniel thought.

Even so, he was tempted. He poured a drop of the smooth pale liquid into a small ceramic glass, took it out onto the terrace, stood it carefully on the tiled table as he sat. He closed his eyes. He dozed. And for a moment he was back when he'd first discovered this haven, this hideaway from his other world, this little house down the steps. This was where he was meant to be; he'd known it from day one. No-one judged you here. They accepted you for yourself, they welcomed you. Sure, they liked the American dollar, but it was more than that. It was genuine.

The first firework was so loud it sounded as though the mountains above had cracked open; he'd forgotten how the Italians loved their fireworks. The sound ricocheted off rock, ebbed away but was then replaced with more bangs, whizzes, stutters of coloured lights as they roared upwards, arched and then fell back to the ground. A pause. Somewhere down near the beach there was cheering. Then they started again.

Daniel sipped the limoncello and it slid down his throat like liquid gold.

New York, America, the world, the TV, the newspaper headlines, the ever-ringing telephone, all the horrors that were part of his life today seemed far away. The fear that was tangible. The funerals, one after another. The sadness. Just getting out of bed each morning was an effort; he could feel himself shrinking, becoming weaker, ageing. His mirror confirmed it.

Here... well, it was as though time had stood still.

Another sip of limoncello. She - Rosa, Lucia, whoever she was – was right. This was something more than special; it was as unique as this tiny, unspoilt village tucked away in the south of Italy beneath the mountains was.

And he was thinking of leaving, never coming back? Had he gone crazy?

THE ART OF MAKING SPAGHETTI

He awoke suddenly to the strangest smell: a combination of cheap perfume – some flower fragrance, Lily of the Valley possibly? – and ice cream. He coughed to give himself time to gather his senses. It was infuriating, this tendency he was developing of falling asleep whenever things were quiet. Certainly he was getting on in years, but dropping off was an old man's weakness; he wasn't old. Not that old. Not yet.

It was hot, though, the air clammy as a flannel, even inside the church with its soaring roof and snowy marble pillars. Hotter still inside the confessional. He blamed his sleepiness on it being August and felt somewhat better.

"*Padre*?" A girl's voice came through the lacework grill, light, hesitant.

"Are you…um... available? I mean, can we talk?"

He could tell at once that she wasn't Italian, though she spoke it well.

"We can, my child. You wish to confess?"

He waited. From outside came the street sounds he knew so well: a blast of opera from a sports car, mothers rounding up straying children. A dog barked half-heartedly.

"No. I mean, *grazie*, but that's not why I'm here. I'd like your advice, please."

The priest sighed, disappointed. So very few people came to him for confession these days. He understood, of course. The village had changed in recent years. Now tourists flocked here from other parts of Italy, from other countries even in search of sea and sun and fun. Beach bars had sprung up like umbrellas, restaurants with checked tablecloths and candles were rife and always crowded. There was even a discotheque, he'd been told, where the music was so loud it numbed your skull, the lights so dazzling you needed to wear dark glasses or risk going blind.

Sins, no doubt about it, must spread like the plague in such places. So how come no-one came to him to be absolved? People came to him for his good, down to earth advice, which yes, was flattering. But what of their spiritual needs?

"If it's advice you want, my child, there's no need for us to sit here in the dark. Let's…"

"No, father. I really would prefer it like this. If you don't mind."

She was shy. He smiled. *Va bene*, let her remain incognito.

"So…?"

He let the word hang there.

"Well." She drew a deep breath. "You see, my parents are English. Church of England too, I suppose, though religion doesn't rate too high on their list of priorities. Anyway, when my father's work brought us to live in Rome, they sent me to a Catholic school. It had a good reputation, and was nearby. It had trees too, forty-three of them, I counted. They were very old."

She paused.

"And though I didn't want to go at first I came to love it. So really, as it's all their fault, you'd think they would understand, wouldn't you? But they don't."

She sniffed and the priest sensed that tears weren't far away. He leaned forward.

"About what, exactly?"

"About my wanting to be a nun."

"Ah." His spirit soared. Here, after all, was an opportunity to achieve something, a reason for having passed so much of each day crammed inside a wooden box, hardly able to breathe. Waiting, hoping.

"And how can I help, my child? I think possibly you want me to suggest ways to bring your parents around?"

"Well, yes."

"There is only one way to do that, you know. That's to be sure in your own heart that it's what you really, truly want. If it is right for you, they'll understand. Maybe not at first, but eventually they'll accept your decision. They'll know that God has called you, and that you have answered."

He heard fidgeting from the other side of the grill, the sound of bangles knocking together as she moved her arm; he imagined her tossing back long hair. Then, a pause.

"But father, how can I be sure?"

So the soul in question was not yet secured. It was hovering above the confessional like a brilliant turquoise butterfly he'd once seen in a book, fluttery, nervous. The priest realised he must reach out and grasp it quickly if it was not to be lost. But it was fragile. Gently does it.

"If you feel the pull of the church..."

"I do, father. I do. I really do. I've thought about it and talked to the nuns, and to God too. For over a year now. And I haven't wavered at all. But..."

But. A very short word that was full of threat, of doubt. Someone in the church coughed, there was whispering, then footsteps heading back towards the main door.

"A few weeks ago, just after we'd arrived, I met this boy. He's from the village. I mean, of course I've known plenty of boys before, but he's different somehow. Special."

A boy. The priest could see him: one of the slim dark youths who were drawn to street corners like pins to magnets, always laughing and joking and punching each other in play. If he was typical of the area he would probably have a lightening temper that would change in a flash to remorse; would give promises and flowers stolen from outside a *pensione* with equal charm, adore children, be addicted to football.

A boy not unlike the boy he himself had been 40 years ago when he too had been grappling with the same decision this girl now faced.

"And he's made you think again, this boy?"

"Oh I haven't told him anything about my intention, father."

"But since knowing him you feel different about wanting to be a nun? Less sure?"

"Yes. And no."

"Which?"

Hearing impatience in his voice, the priest checked himself. He must go carefully. Here was a girl who wanted to become the bride of Christ, who had made the huge and difficult decision to turn her back on the things most girls dream about: a husband, a home, children, and more. A car, pretty dresses, a colour television. He'd heard you could buy a special contraption to record the television programmes you couldn't watch at the time they were on, or wanted to watch again.

Such a materialistic world, it was becoming. Things were the only thing that mattered. And yet, the priest had to admit to finding such frivolities fascinating.

"No. How could I possibly change my mind after… after everything."

The girl spoke with quiet determination, her voice controlled. Anyone else, anyone unused to dealing with people, to hearing what they say in the silences between their words, would have believed her.

The priest closed his eyes and muttered a prayer. Tell me, God. What shall I say? He waited for a reply, a sign, something.

Nothing. The church was silent now, empty. He imagined he could hear the mouse scuttling behind the confessional, the one he put a few breadcrumbs down for each night before he locked up.

So it was up to him. He made his decision.

"Do you know" he asked "that there are machines with which you can make spaghetti, the strands so long and fine they could have been made by hand?"

The girl stifled a giggle.

"Of course I do, father."

"Have you ever used one?"

"Well, no."

"You asked for my opinion and I'll give it. But, my child, it's no more than an opinion. Eventually only you can make up your mind."

He sensed her bend closer to the grill.

"I understand, father. So what then, what d'you think I should do?"

"I think you should learn the art of making spaghetti. With one of these new-fangled machines, of course. You should, let's see… go water skiing. Have you ever tried that? It looks fun. I think you should take a steam train across India – they still have them there, I believe. Or at least see a film about what it's like to ride in one. Do you like dogs? Take in a couple of strays, give them love, fuss them. All living creatures need love, you know."

He paused.

"How about music? Do you play an instrument? If not, pick one, give it a try. I hear the bassoon is a bit neglected these days. Walk barefoot in snow. Grow something exotic, not cannabis of course, something pretty or edible. And… I don't know. Think of your own challenges."

He could put it off no longer.

"Oh, and you should maybe get to know this young man of yours better, too. Find out just how special he is."

"Really? You really think I should?"

The priest couldn't help but smile at the relief in her voice.

"Then, when you've done all these things and more, think again about becoming a nun. Maybe you'll know it's the right path for you. I hope so. But maybe you'll have discovered that God has other plans for you. And that will be alright too."

More people had come into the church, tourists muttering praises of the chandeliers, the sparkling altar, stopping to drop coins in the collection box. Before the priest could continue the girl spoke.

"Father, can I ask you something? I mean... you don't have to answer. But have you ever regretted your decision to give your life to the church?"

The old man held back a chuckle. The cheek of the girl. He was flattered too; it was the first time in years that anyone had asked about him.

"Yes. And no," he replied. And now he gave a small laugh that even to him sounded strange. He should laugh more often. "All I can say is that now, at this moment, I don't regret it. Not at all."

"God bless you, father. And many, many thanks."

She was gone before he could reply. And somehow the church seemed emptier than ever. He was torn between doubt and satisfaction; though later, alone in the stark white room behind the altar, a book open on his lap, unread, he found himself recalling their conversation. By and large, he decided, he had said the right things. He hoped God would agree.

And now it was up to her.

Sunday morning mass was the best attended of all, though hardly crowded, most of the faces familiar: elderly locals following the habit of a lifetime, scrunched up men, fat women in black, a grandchild on each side until they grew old enough to find other things to do on Sunday mornings.

The priest recognised her at once. She sat near the front, her hair red and crinkled, pale skin freckled, hands clasped neatly in her lap. With her was a boy he recognised, though he couldn't put a name to the face; he forgot so many things these days. He wouldn't forget the girl in a hurry though. She'd done as much for him as he had for her. And after the mass, shaking hands at the door, his congregation now anxious to get on with the rest of the day, he waited for her, wanting to say something special, something appropriate, he didn't know what.

She beat him to it.

"*Buon appetito*, father. Have a good lunch." Her smile said the rest.

RAVELLO

The station at Naples was a surprise. She recalled it as being dirty, litter everywhere; now it gleamed. Even the gypsies seemed to have been smartened up. They wore clothes that were flamboyant in primary colours, the kind you could buy – if you could afford them – from chic ethnic shops off the King's Road.

Two gypsy women and a small girl were sitting at a table in the station restaurant eating pasta, sipping wine from long-stemmed glasses. Helen wasn't hungry, which was just as well. Her connecting train was due to depart in 15 minutes. She did fancy some fruit though. Was there time to look outside? She decided yes, finding the heat a shock after the cool interior of the station.

Slipping between parked cars, a small suitcase in each hand, she was conscious of perspiration trickling down between her shoulder blades.

"*Vuoi un taxi?*" she was asked three times, but kept shaking her head.

Then fingers gripped her arm. "*Scusa. Parli italiano?*"

He was tall, clean shaven, wore a crisp white shirt. He didn't seem like someone trying to pick her up. "Just a little," she said.

What he needed, he explained, were volunteers to give blood. For the poor of the city. He pointed to a small caravan parked to one side. Wouldn't she like to help save the life of a child hit by a drunken driver, or a mother in childbirth?

"I'm sorry, I have to catch a train."

It sounded feeble, but it was true. Besides, the caravan looked tiny, claustrophobic. She would be taking a risk; the needle might be dirty, she could become infected, end up in hospital herself. You had to be so careful.

"Ten minutes." He held up his hands, fingers splayed. He had a dazzling smile.

Helen wondered what she would have said if he'd been inviting her for a drink. Would she have been tempted to catch a later train?

"I haven't got ten minutes."

He shrugged, defeated. "Well, have a good journey," he said, and was off, eyes skinned for someone else to approach.

She had to run now, just catching the train that would take her to Sorrento. From there she would catch a bus to Amalfi, from there another bus up through the mountains to Ravello. Or – if it was late, if she was hungry and tired and desperate for a shower – she might take a taxi from Amalfi. It would be expensive, but a more appropriate way to arrive.

Ravello had style, elegance. In summer there was a week of recitals attended by the famous – film stars, politicians, writers. They would sit under the trees wearing diamonds that out-glittered those in the black sky overhead and listen to Wagner.

You don't – if you can help it – arrive in Ravello by bus.

Although she'd arrived by bus last time, in June two years ago. June: the very best month to be in southern Italy, the guide books said, when the perfume of flowers is everywhere, the air soft and balmy, and the nights just made for romance.

How could she be held responsible for what had happened? She's been on holiday with her mother. Her father had died suddenly – a heart attack while he was watching TV, laughing actually at 'Allo 'Allo which everyone agreed was a good way to go– and her mother needed sunshine, wine, new faces, to bring her back to life. Helen had accompanied her.

He, Sergio, had been working as a tour guide along the Amalfi coast. Born in Ravello, he still lived in the village, though it meant a lot of to-ing and fro-ing.

"It's good to come home each night to peace, to clean air," he'd told her.

His eyes were the colour of hazelnuts. He wasn't young, at least not young enough to be considered a *pappagallo*, one of the arrogant young men whose sole purpose in life was seducing women. *Fare amore.* It was such a beautiful expression for something that really was no different from what the stray dogs did in the street, sniffing each other, circling, jeered at by all the locals.

"Yobs," her mother had called them, always on the side of the dogs. "Stupid, insensitive yobs."

Sergio was sensitive. He was polite, too, and funny. And sad. He'd been married, he told her. For four years, three months, six days. His wife had died in a car crash on the tortuous road that zig-zagged down to the coast.

"It was her fault, witnesses said. I believe it, she always drove too fast."

Helen had hoped he wouldn't go into details, was worried about what she could say. He hadn't.

Instead, he'd talked about his life since then. His English was perfect; he'd lived in Harrogate for a year, helping out in an uncle's restaurant, attending classes in the evening.

He still wanted to improve, he said, so she must feel free to correct him.

And she had, as they'd strolled round the gardens of the Villa Cimbrone, along rose-arboured walks that led to panoramic views of more mountains, valleys, the sea stretching out ahead into the silvery distance.

"Africa is over there," he'd said, pointing, one hand resting on her shoulder.

Even when he'd removed it she'd felt it still, heavy, warm.

Then he took her to eat at a restaurant tucked away off a courtyard, a tiny place where everyone knew him.

"This is good," he'd said, pointing to the menu. "*Spaghetti alle vongole*. Some places cheat and use frozen mussels, but here they are fresh."

"Cheat," she'd said, emphasising the E sound. He'd said chit. He'd repeated it after her, watching her lips carefully, intently.

She'd excused herself, stood to go to the Ladies, not so much because she needed to but because she'd wanted to check that she was looking her best for him, that her hair was still smooth and that her lipstick didn't need touching up.

He made her feel beautiful, though she wasn't, she knew that. She was nothing special at all.

The glow in her eyes had startled her.

"You know something?" her mother had said over breakfast. "I do believe this holiday is doing you as much good as it is me." Helen had reached for her fruit juice.

When, inevitably, Sergio had made love to her, it was as natural as if they'd simply been smiling at each other.

"*T'amo*," he'd said and it didn't sound false or trite, like something from an Italian pop song.

"Stay with me," he'd said, the night before she'd departed. She'd reached for her wine glass which was empty, spun it slowly on the cotton cloth.

"I can't."

"You don't love me enough?" There was a pleading note in his voice and for a moment she'd felt angry. Why was he doing this to her? He knew the situation, he'd said he understood.

"I love you. But I love my husband too."

There had been a sudden flurry of birds, and she had recalled stories she'd heard of huntsmen, guns blasting, of a countryside devoid of birds. The stories were wrong. She'd turned her head to the open window to watch their graceful flight. The evening sky was mauve.

"You are lucky," he told her. "You love two men and they both love you."

"No, I'm not lucky," she'd said, dismayed at the single tear that was sliding down the side of her nose.

He'd reached across and wiped it away with his thumb.

She'd left at seven the next morning, and was soon back in wet, green and chilly England. She'd felt guilty twice over: once for being unfaithful to Ben, who deserved much better, once for abandoning her lover who'd already had his fair share of life's blows.

Sergio had asked her to come back, had begged her. He would wait. They would be together one day, he'd said, he knew it.

Helen smiled now, remembering, thinking how she'd wanted to tell him not to bank on it, but she couldn't think of the words in Italian. He'd been right anyway: she was back.

She'd booked a room at the same *pensione* as she'd stayed in before – a converted monastery with high-ceilinged corridors and Moorish arches, everything white. She recognised at once the lemony smell of the place.

"*Benvenuto, signora.*"

Even the dark, unsmiling woman who came forward to shake her hand was the same. She could almost have been a nun, someone left over from a time when the only sound was the singing of vespers, the soft scuffling of shoes on tiled floors. The place was very quiet now; it was early in the season, of course.

Behind the desk stood a young man in his twenties with curly black hair. The woman's son? Like hers, his expression was sombre, though as Helen turned to follow the woman, he winked at her. Such eyelashes, Helen thought, with envy.

Her room was tiny, a cell. Though comfortable enough it felt austere, needed something to bring it to life – pictures, colour. Flowers, Helen decided. She would pick some later, would ask for a vase.

Sergio had brought her flowers: pale cream roses with thick petals that were cool to touch. She'd pressed one, crushing it beneath a telephone directory she'd sneaked from reception. Hating to sacrifice it but wanting so much to take back with her something from that time, something tangible.

Ben never gave her flowers.

He paid the mortgage, the bills, gave her money for the hairdresser, her painting classes, new curtains when she insisted the old ones were fading. He loved her in his undemonstrative way, and she knew it. The flower thing had never bothered her, until now.

The shutters were stiff but eventually she opened them. Below was the garden, a tangle of brambles and weeds; and beyond it the small square that was the heart of the village with its church, bars and a line of taxis sheltering under the trees.

She would shower, change into something fresh, a blue cheesecloth dress she'd bought specially for the trip. Sergio was always saying how he liked her in blue. Then she would go to a bar for a drink. And from the bar, she would telephone him. His number was as familiar to her as her own, even though she'd hardly used it: a couple of times when she'd been in Ravello, and then a couple more from England when she'd first returned home, surreptitious, brief, wanting just to hear him say that he loved her still and that he was waiting for her.

He'd never rung her, of course.

Gradually she'd put him to the back of her mind, not forgotten – how could she? – but tucked away. His phone number had been like a stash of money kept in reserve for times of emergency. She knew that all she had to do was pick up the telephone and dial it to hear the sound of his voice.

The bar was almost empty, a ceiling fan spinning listlessly, the Gaggia shushing.

"*Punt E Mes, per favore.*"

Helen used to drink Campari until Sergio introduced her to *Punt E Mes*. She drank it because it was his favourite drink.

I'm like a schoolgirl with a crush, she thought to herself.

She asked too for a *gettone*, turning it between her fingers. Savouring the moment when she would slip it into the phone and dial his number. And she'd hear his voice, full of surprise and pleasure. He'd always sounded delighted when she'd phoned.

There was no answer.

Strange; early evenings used to be the best time to find him at home. Still, he could be anywhere, caught up in a problem with clients, or a traffic jam. She would leave it now and try again later.

Suddenly she noticed that the bar was filling up. Men mostly – she saw the one from the *pensione* who nodded and muttered *buona sera*. Chairs were produced from a back room, arranged in rows. The television that was suspended above the bar was switched on. It was when she heard the word *calcio* that the penny dropped. Football. Of course. Italy must be playing Helen realised; all around her excitement buzzed like a trapped bumble bee.

Damn, Helen thought. She'd wanted to sit there in the cool, sipping her drink, trying the telephone every now and again until he answered. Anticipating the moment. Now she would have to move on.

She would go and eat. The *trattoria* she chose also had a television set high in a corner. It too was switched on, figures scuttling back and forth, a quiet roar of hundreds of voices suddenly soaring in excitement. The waiter watched from the corner of his eye as he waited to take Helen's order, his attention elsewhere as she asked about the asparagus, whether the new season's crop was in yet.

"*Cosa?*" There was impatience in his voice.

She said never mind, ordered a salad.

The other diners were as keen to watch the game as the waiter, some even turned their chairs round so they could see better. Helen felt bored. Seemed like men the world over were obsessed with football, even here in Ravello. She didn't get it. She couldn't stand the game, a lot of mud covered men racing around after a ball, yelling at each other, their fans shouting or fighting, often both. She'd made a point of avoiding it, which wasn't difficult, Ben wasn't bothered about it either.

But never mind about Ben. Where on earth was Sergio? She'd tried him twice more, again in the bar and then from the unpleasant smelling phone booth outside.

Of course, she thought, he might be watching the football with friends, a crowd of them crammed into a room, drinking beer and eating pizza. It didn't seem the kind of thing he'd do; she remembered listening to music with him, talking about books: Pirandello, Moravia and his stories of Rome. She'd teased him about being very patriotic in his reading.

Just the same, maybe even he felt passionate about football. She'd never asked him. There were a lot of things she'd never asked him,

The game seemed to go on forever. Then, finally, it was over. Italy had won.

The world outside exploded: there were shouts, cheers, car horns were beeped, fireworks splattered the sky, the mountains echoing the bangs and fizzes so that it was impossible to speak. Eventually Helen paid her bill and left, weaving her way through the crowd of excited revellers, heading back to the peace of her *pensione.* Nearly there, she passed the bar again, quieter now; there were more people out on the streets than inside.

She would have one more drink, one more go at the telephone.

She was about to give up when a party of Italians arrived, settled at a nearby table, among them a man and a woman she was sure she recognised. She and Sergio had spent some time with them. If she was right, they both spoke excellent English.

As she approached them conversation stopped, everyone looked up. Then the man smiled.

"*Signora!*" He stood up, caught her hand. "I remember your face so well but not, I'm afraid, your name..."

She introduced herself.

"*Si, si. Adesso mi ricordo.* Come, please join us for a drink."

He beckoned the water, then pulled a seat from another table over to theirs.

For the first time since she'd arrived, Helen felt almost happy. They remembered her. This was what she'd come back for.

"I only arrived this evening," she said. "Haven't yet had time to ring Sergio." She didn't know why she lied. Maybe she didn't want to admit to being too keen.

"Sergio?"

The husband and wife exchanged glances.

"But he's not here. Didn't you know?" It was the wife who spoke. Helen felt something plummet inside her. She should have phoned him from home, should have checked that he wasn't off on some trip.

"Do you know when he'll be back?" she asked.

The man leant forward.

"He got married over a year ago. To a girl from the north. He's living up there now, Volterra, one of those beautiful hill towns, you know it maybe?"

"It was time," the wife said. "He needed a woman, a family."

Helen knew she had to make an effort, had to make conversation as though she were just catching up with news of a mutual friend.

"He has ... he has a family?"

"Just one child so far. A baby boy, I think."

Helen downed what was left of her drink in one go. She couldn't believe he hadn't waited for her. He'd said he would. He'd promised.

"And you, how are things with you?" The man tipped his head, waiting.

"And your husband, is he well? Wasn't he ... wait a minute, let me think. A solicitor? Am I right?"

Helen's voice, when she replied, was so faint she had to repeat her words. "We're separated. Last winter. He found someone new."

"*Non e possibile!*" He looked genuinely upset.

"But what an idiot. Still, a beautiful young woman like you, you'll soon meet another man, a better one. Find yourself an Italian, we Italian men are…"

His wife caught his eye, shook her head, the slightest movement but Helen saw it. She managed a smile.

"So. When you next speak to Sergio, please say hello from me,"

She stayed as long as felt polite, then made her excuses, said she was tired after the journey. They said of course. They were probably relieved.

The streets were quieter now, the sky almost dark, a few widely spaced streetlights making pools. Dazed, unwilling to go to bed yet, Helen wandered around the back alleyways absorbing everything, so many smells and sounds reminding her of last time. And children, there were still a few ignoring calls to go indoors, that it was bedtime, that if they didn't go in right this minute they'd get *uno schiaffo*, a slap.

So Sergio had a baby boy.

She and Sergio had never talked about children. If they had, that would have been it, their relationship would have withered instantly. Why hadn't she thought? Most Italian men want a family – they're wonderful with children, naturals at being dads. Besides, it was proof of their virility. It had been ten years ago, more, that she'd discovered for sure she couldn't have a baby. And after the initial shock and disappointment, and that awful feeling that she was a failure, she'd accepted the news and put it to the back of her mind. Ben had helped. He'd been wonderful, in fact, said it didn't matter, that they had each other, that having a family was a nice option but not the only life they could lead. Had he lied? Was that why he eventually fell out of love with her and in love with someone else?

A football dropped over a high wall, landed in front of her, rolled towards the gutter. She picked it up, turned to the wrought-iron gate that was swinging open, a boy in shorts and T-shirt peering round, hesitant. Now he walked slowly towards her.

"Here, don't look so worried, it didn't hit me," she said in hesitant Italian. He reached, took the ball from her.

"Grazie signora." A quick grin and he was gone, but not before she'd noticed his right hand, a number of fingers missing. An accident, she supposed. Many of the local children helped their parents doing manual work from a very early age: carrying things, scrubbing floors with chemical cleaners, using hammers and knives that you wouldn't let a child near back home. Using machinery. Accidents were far more common than they ought to be.

Sergio had said that once. She'd forgotten. That Ravello may be stunningly beautiful for visitors, a utopia, but that it was a hard life for the people who worked behind the scenes to keep it that way.

For some reason the young man at the station came to mind. Would he still be there, still looking for volunteers to donate blood? You may save a child's life, he'd said. Wasn't that something worth doing, and so easy too? She'd look out for him when she went home.

The empty night streets clicked with the sound of her heels as finally she gave up and went back to her *pensione*. The same young man was behind the desk. As she came through the open doors he stifled a yawn, turned to the board behind him and took down her keys.

"You have had a good evening, *signora?* Is there anything you need?"

If only it was that easy, she thought. I thought I needed Sergio, but now I'm not so sure. It was a dream I fell in love with as much as a man. A beautifully packaged dream of a place where the sun always shines, the sea glitters, where there are violins and fine wines, and everyone smiles all the time.

Stupid, stupid idiot, she thought. Life isn't like that, not even in Ravello. It's real here too. It's what you make it, wherever you are.

Face it, she told herself. You've probably had a narrow escape. Time to go home, start again.

"No thank you," she said. Then an idea came to her.

"Yes, there is something. You like football?"

He hesitated.

"*Si, Certo.*"

"So can you please explain to me what it is that makes it so exciting to watch?"

He looked as though she was teasing, but then grinned.

"With pleasure, *signora*. Here, take a seat. I get us some beer – you like beer? Good. Then I tell you about tonight's game, yes? You know, it started slowly, we thought this is bad, Italy will lose, but then just before half time…"

Listening to his voice, watching his hands, so animated, the joy in his face as he talked, Helen felt a calm come over her. Everything was going to be alright. She was never going to love football, but she was going to be alright.

THE WOMAN WHO LOVED TO PLAY GAMES

A man had died just an hour ago. Young – well, thirtyish – newly arrived from Milwaukee or somewhere and probably jet lagged. That's what they said. He'd sat on a roadside wall, put his feet up on it, twisted to look out over the sea. He had sandals, white socks, white legs. They noticed that kind of thing, the people sitting at tables outside the cafe opposite drinking their morning *cappuccinos*. One moment he was there, head lifted as he watched a seagull, the next he'd vanished, tipped backwards and crashed down the other side onto the steps that led steeply down to the beach.

Cracked his skull. Died instantly. Blood splashed everywhere.

Beth hugged the bag of warm pastries to her as she hurried up the steps back to their *pensione*, to where Jacqui would be sitting by the open window in her faded kimono, waiting. It was only mid-morning but she'd already be needing sustenance, something sweet to give her a boost of energy. Jacqui ate constantly. But Beth didn't mind, nor did she mind being a go-for.

Today she was bringing back something special: news of a real-life drama.

Jacqui took a bite of a squidgy doughnut. Custard oozed down her fingers.

"Mmm. Scrummy."

Her rosy tongue whisked sugar from her top lip. Another bite.

"But what a terrible thing to happen. Poor man. And for his family too. Was he with someone?"

Beth nodded.

"His wife. She was in their hotel room, unpacking probably, that's the first thing wives do when they arrive, isn't it? There was an argument about who was going to go and tell her what had happened. No-one wanted to. They tossed a coin."

"Oh don't. I mean, that's not the kind of news you want to be getting at the start of your holiday."

"Or at the end."

"Hmm. Not so sure about that." Jacqui held the remaining pastry out to Beth - who shook her head - before tearing it in two.

"A couple of weeks together, in each other's company twenty-four hours a day?" she said through a mouthful of pastry. "That's bad news for a lot of marriages. If they were about to head home I'd be suspicious. Had he been driven to suicide? Was he drugged? Hypnotised?"

The two women exchanged a glance, then both of them giggled.

"Just imagine what Pat would do with it, a story like this. Of course he'd have been murdered, and knowing the way her mind works, he wouldn't have deserved it. There'd have been a misunderstanding, a slight one, nothing serious. But his wife decided he had to be punished. She'd get clean away with it too."

"Pat loves that, doesn't she?" Beth said. "Playing games. Twisting things. Writing novels where the innocent victim not only doesn't get justice but comes off even worse at the end."

"Like in Ripley's Game, remember? That poor young man with what was it? Leukaemia?"

"And what about the one where the dog gets kidnapped?" Beth bent down to search for the sandals she'd kicked off minutes before. "That was horrible. So unfair."

She crossed to the window scratching her arm gently, last night's crop of mosquito bites. She'd counted seven new ones.

"It's odd. You know you shouldn't enjoy reading stories like that. But you do. Wonder why?"

Jacqui stood, stretched.

"Cos people are nasty pieces of work. Right. If we're going to do any sightseeing today I'd better get dressed."

She slipped off her kimono and moved across to where her skirt lay scrunched up at the bottom of her bed. Beth - unused to seeing naked bodies, especially one as voluptuous as Jacqui's - was amazed at the satin smoothness of skin stretched tight over rounded flesh, the darkness and size of her nipples.

She turned away and gazed up at the white sky.

Beth rarely even looked at her own naked body in the mirror.

"So. On with our Pat pilgrimage," she said. "Via Monte first? And then, the beach."

Number fifteen Via Monte was tucked back off the steps and hard to see, the walls topped with swathes of greenery that would later be dotted with vivid purple flowers.

"That's the trouble with being here early in the season," Jacqui had said. "It's like arriving at a party to find they're still spearing pineapple cubes, and chilling the Cinzano in the sink."

"It's just right for me," Beth replied. "It's so green and lush. And it's plenty hot enough - come on, this is a midsummer's day back home."

They stood on tiptoe, pressed their noses against the wrought iron gate, could just see the grey domed roof.

"Well? What d'you think?"

"Of the house? Looks alright, but nothing special. You'd think they'd have a plaque outside, wouldn't you?"

Jacqui could imagine it.

"The writer – no, wait - the American writer Patricia Highsmith – should it say bestselling? – anyway, lived here in Positano in … whenever it was… 1960 something… whilst working on her psychological thriller, The Glass Cell."

"Though how she could produce something so grim in such a stunning place, I can't imagine." Beth pulled a face.

"She was depressed."

"She was always depressed."

"True. I wonder if she's happier now? Can't remember where she's living. Switzerland I think."

There was a shuffling in the undergrowth, a tiny squeak.

"Oh look, Jacqui." Beth dropped down onto her knees, held out her fingers and a skinny black cat edged nervously towards her. It gazed at her through sticky eyes.

"Isn't she gorgeous?"

"And hungry. Got kits too by the look of her."

"D'you think she's a stray?"

"They all are."

"What about the people who live in the house?"

"It's probably only used for a couple of months in summer."

"Poor poppet." Beth stood, tried the gate but it was locked. "When we come back up I'm going to bring her some food. I'll bring something tomorrow too, and the day after."

"And once we've gone home, what then?"

"I don't care. At least I can help while we're here."

Beth brushed gravel from her knees. She had a sudden thought. Smiled.

"It's what Pat would have done, isn't it? She adored cats."

Turning, Beth could see down over the houses to the sea beyond, a grey pebbly beach and then a strip of sand, the water fringed with little black insect-like figures.

"So how about this swim?"

She was enjoying the sea more than she'd imagined she would, the freedom she felt as she sliced effortlessly through the turquoise water. She used to swim in the public pool, took the bus to town, never minded the long journey, until he'd decided he needed her help in the shop. Him: smirking, arrogant Uncle Ronald with his fat yellow fingers and greasy hair, his smell of stale cigarettes and WD40. As soon as she left school he'd insisted, though she knew nothing about hardware and didn't want to. Your aunt could do with a bit more help around the house too, he'd said. She's not getting any younger. Have you seen the state of her knees? It wouldn't hurt you to go shopping sometimes either, or iron my shirts.

Payback time, that's what he called it. We took you in when there was no-one else, looked after you all these years.

Who asked you to? she'd wanted to scream. I'd have been better off in an orphanage. Better still, dead.

"Looks like the beach is getting busy," she said now. "We don't want those awful sunchairs at the back."

"Let's go. We can pick up some pizza slices on the way down."

Beth couldn't believe how lucky she was to be here, with someone as wonderful as Jacqui, away from home for the first time ever. Jacqui had changed her life in so many ways, and now this. It was incredible.

Evenings were mosquito time.

Before they left their room they both of them sprayed their bare legs, arms, necks, even down their cleavages with insect repellent. Beth choked on the smell, wished she could be wearing some exotic perfume like that spicy Opium that Jacqui always wore back home – chosen, she said, because it had caused such a controversy when it was launched, though Beth didn't really know what she meant. It could never compete with your insect repellent though, Jacqui said. So they shared the can of spray even though Jacqui didn't need it. So far she hadn't been bitten once.

"They like nice blonde English girls," she'd said. "Like the Italian men, always following you with their come-to-bed eyes."

"They're not."

Jacqui laughed, ran her hand down the length of Beth's hair, hesitated the briefest moment as her fingertips brushed against her neck.

"What, with your long yellow hair, and all those freckles? Of course they are, And why not? You're gorgeous. You, my girl, have spent too long in that dreary backwater with that creepy uncle of yours."

"You're right about that."

Beth hated it there, hated everything about it: the claustrophobic streets with their ugly brick houses, grubby net curtains drawn. The people, drab and unfriendly, grey people under a grey sky, and everywhere the smell of boiled greens and stagnant water.

"It is a bit of a backwater, isn't it?"

"A bit? It's so dead that it doesn't even have a proper library of its own. Without books people shrivel and die, or at least, they might as well."

Beth laughed.

"But if we'd had a library we wouldn't have needed a mobile one," she said. "And then I wouldn't have seen it driving past and would never have discovered Pat's books, and all those other fantastic writers."

"And me, don't forget. You wouldn't have met me."

"And you of course." Beth nodded. "You don't know how I look forward to Fridays, every other week, that walk down to the patch of scrubland they call a park, can you believe? And that big white van waiting..."

Jacqui emptied her glass. Beth followed her example.

"And we wouldn't be sitting here now, sipping... what's this wine called? I've forgotten again."

She was definitely getting into the swing of drinking. Of drinking a lot. To think, not long ago she'd have thought it outrageous to have more than two Babychams.

"*Vino della casa*. Another carafe?"

They went most evenings to the same *trattoria*, a small family-run place, not posh, nothing fancy, but the seafood was unlike anything they'd had before. After the first time they were welcomed like old friends: the waiter grinning, ushering them to a corner table - their corner table - putting down cutlery and thick white napkins. The chef would put his head through the hatch, smile, wave *ciao*; the portions were definitely getting bigger.

Afterwards they would need to walk it off, usually heading along the esplanade – ignoring the music coming from the nightclub, the flickering lights, the calls to come and see from the doorman - and then onto the beach at the far end where the mountains reached down to the water. It was another place after dark, empty, wild, the water now navy blue, ripples picked up by moonlight. They walked silently, shoes swinging from their fingers, the sand cool between their toes.

As they passed close to a cluster of large rocks they heard a sudden giggle, saw glimpses of movement, the white of a bare leg that was quickly withdrawn. A man's voice – husky, controlled - muttered something in Italian, a girl whispered a reply. Pebbles shifted under moving bodies.

Jacqui turned quickly away towards the water.

"Over-rated I think, don't you?" she said after a bit.

"What?"

"Sex with a man."

Beth didn't reply.

"I nearly got married, you know." Jacqui slowed down. "A few years ago. He was OK. Tall, played cricket, had an infectious laugh. Had a good salary too. But luckily I came to my senses. I don't think I'm the marrying kind, just the idea makes me feel trapped."

Still Beth said nothing. Jacqui stopped.

"You have... I mean, you're not still a virgin, are you?"

"Course not." Beth dug her toes into the sand. "I've had boyfriends. Two or three. But... well, he disapproves of course"

"Uncle Ronald? He disapproves of everything."

They'd reached the sea. Beth kicked at the warm water, gently at first and then splashing it high so that her skirt hem was soon saturated.

"He does. He's a nasty, hateful, miserable old sod."

Jacqui glanced towards her but said nothing.

They'd planned what they would do each day. Next morning it was a trip to Sorrento. It was early when they arrived at the bus stop on the curve in the road near the bar, but already there was a continuous stream of cars, bikes, scooters, Other tourists in shorts and straw hats clustered near the stop with them; a few locals in black and clutching shopping bags had stationed themselves at the front. Everyone was looking out for the first sign of the blue Sita bus edging towards them along the coast road, listening for the loud hooting at every corner that echoed from the cliffs above, so loud it could be heard out at sea,

When eventually it arrived it was packed. They had to stand most of the way, clinging to the rails above their heads, enjoying being swung around. Beth said it was like an Alton Towers ride. A woman with yellow hair and dark glasses was sick most of the way, sat clutching a paper bag in one hand, tissues in the other. Exchanging a glance, Beth and Jacqui edged away from her.

Finally they tumbled out of the bus, hot and yet anxious to see whatever there was to see. Jacqui thought it was like a film set: golden walled buildings, grand hotels, heavy wooden doors draped with greenery, dark sinister doorways. The main piazza led onto a web of narrow alleyways lined with shops selling leather bags, strings of garlic, inlaid woodwork, laces said to have been handmade by old ladies up in the mountains.

"The usual tat," Jacqui said. "Probably made in China."

She caught hold of Beth's hand, pushed a way through the dawdling crowds.

"Or we'll lose each other," she said over her shoulder, twining their fingers more tightly.

She wanted to keep Beth moving, knew that she was getting upset about the animals. The tired and skinny horses pulling carriages, flanks sweating as they clipped along, heads held low. The cats who spat and shot off whenever Beth tried to pet them. The scraps of dogs stretched out along walls, under anything that offered shade, dusty and lifeless.

One lying between some over flowing bins was bleeding from a badly mangled leg.

Beth hesitated, but was tugged past.

"How can people here be so cruel?"

"They're not as bad as some. In South Korea they eat cats and dogs."

Beth's eyes opened wide.

"They don't,"

"Pat said it in an interview. She said that's why she hates them."

They came to a halt in front of a palette of bright colours that was a fruit and vegetable display.

"Look at that," Jacqui said,pointing, changing the subject. "Isn't it ugly? Like an apricot with the pox."

The seller caught her eye.

"*Nespole. Sono dolci.*" He held out a small handful. "*Assaggia.*"

"He wants us to try them."

They took one each, juice squirted, some of it running down Beth's chin so that Jacqui turned her to face her, used a thumb to dab at it.

"Strange taste. But think I could grow to like it."

"Me too. Let's get some."

They were still sticky fingered when finally they found what they'd both been hoping for: a bookshop. Licking off the last of the juice they pushed through the heavy glass door. Inside it was cool, white walled, books beautifully displayed, neatly arranged, row after row of them. Though most were in Italian they couldn't resist taking them down for the joy of handling them, of seeing crisp print against a stark white page, of cover designs that – no matter what the book was about - frequently featured a pretty woman, usually only half dressed.

"Guess that's what sells books here."

"D'you think they have Mary stripping on the front of the Bible?"

"Shh. Jacqui, you can't say that!" Beth shook her head, turned away. And then.

"Look!"

She picked up a hardback, held it up in front of her.

Il talento di Mr Ripley. Wow. Doesn't it sound wonderful in Italian?"

"Shall we get it?"

"Let me see. My God, at that price? That's ridiculous. That's dinner tonight."

"And a carafe of wine."

"You're right. Put it back. We've got to watch the spending."

The cloisters were cool, a welcome relief from the hubbub of the world outside. Jacqui said it was like immersing yourself in an ice cream. The ones they'd bought to eat slowly were melting far too quickly, creamy pearls dropping onto the flagstones as they sat licking like crazy. The book was put safely between them on the stone bench. They'd agreed that they couldn't understand a word of it, but that didn't matter. They knew the story anyway.

"You've read all her novels, haven't you? Bet you can remember every plot, the names of every character..."

Jacqui pulled a face that said don't be silly.

"Thirteen, or fourteen. Most of them anyway. Hopefully she'll do plenty more, though she's getting on a bit now, in her sixties at least."

A little girl in a blue dress ran across the central square trying to kick the pigeons. She tripped on the uneven paving, hesitated, then drew in a big breath and started screaming.

There was a flurry of concern, she was scooped up, hugged, kissed, taken off.

"Spoilt brat," Jacqui muttered.

The quiet returned, settled like dust.

"Heaven," she sighed.

"Jacqui," Beth said. Hesitated.

"You're not going to start again, I hope?"

"I still can't believe I'm here and it's all thanks to…"

"How many more times? I've been wanting to do this trip for years. When I spotted the package tour offer – well, I'd have been crazy not to take it. I thought you'd enjoy it. I certainly am. You don't need to keep…"

"I'll pay you back."

"I know."

"Every penny. I've already saved a bit from the pathetic sum he gives me, and I'm going to …"

"Beth. Shut up."

"Right. I will." She crumbled the end of her cornet and threw it down for the waiting pigeons. "Just as long as you…"

"That's it. I'm off."

Jacqui jumped up and hurried through the cloisters towards the exit, sandals slapping the flagstones. Beth followed her, remembered, turned back for the abandoned book.

Next morning, and something was definitely different. They'd become used to the sun, expected it to be there when they opened the shutters. But not today. It wasn't cold, not at all, but the sky was a heavy grey lid and the plants in the garden were slick with rain.

It was a day for drinking, Jacqui decided. You have to allocate one day for getting pissed, don't you?

Beth could never quite believe Jacqui was a librarian. Even if she only worked in a stuffy box of a van, and seemed to be most admired by the locals for her ability to manoeuvre it in and out of impossible gaps. And look at the way she spelt her name. To Beth – at least until now – librarians were elderly, spindly, wore glasses and cardigans, and never raised their voices above a whisper. Let alone swore.

First, then, coffees at the bar at the top.

Then a quick run down to the next bar - plastic macs held overhead like sails – for an aperitif. *Panini al formaggio* for lunch; the cheese was a bit dry so they needed a brandy to wash it down.

Outside the bar people scuttled past, some huddling under giant umbrellas, youngsters not caring that their hair was sticking to their necks, their feet squelching in soggy sandals. Beth and Jacqui debated going down to a beach bar, decided against, headed instead back to their room for a siesta. It's what people do here, Jacqui said. After lunch everything closes for a few hours.

They'd only just unlocked their door when Beth stopped.

"Is it the seventh or eighth today?"

"Seventh I think."

"I'd completely lost track. OK – so it's my birthday"

"Are you serious?" Beth nodded. Jacqui scowled.

"Why didn't you warn me? That is so mean of you. I haven't got you anything and..."

"I don't want anything."

Jacqui picked up the plastic mac she'd just dropped into the bath, shook it, put it on again.

"You have to have something. Everyone does on their birthday, it's the rules. Stay there. I won't be long."

"Jacqui, where are you off to now? Wait, I'll come."

"Leave this room and I'll be furious."

Beth held up her hands.

"OK, OK."

The door slammed.

It was over an hour before Jacqui returned clutching a small cardboard box. It had a pink ribbon around it, holes in the sides, and when Beth took it from her she was sure she felt something move inside.

"Open it slowly."

Beth put it beside her on the bed, tugged the ribbon free, opened the lid a crack. There was something green inside. She lifted the lid completely. Lettuce leaves. A heap of fresh bright green lettuce leaves.

"Is this dinner?" she asked, not knowing what else it could be.

"Yes. But not for us."

"I don't understand. For the cat?"

"Silly. Course not. Think."

Hesitantly Beth picked up a soft, moist leaf, turned it over.

"Right. A clue. Why are we here?" Jacqui liked her guessing games. Beth didn't, she could never get what Jacqui was on about.

"We're on holiday?"

"And?"

"Mmm." A thought was blossoming. "A Pat pilgrimage."

"So...?"

At that moment Beth saw it: a spiral shell the colour of sand, beneath it a single muscular pad, contracting as the creature edged along.

"Snails! You got me a snail."

Jacqui grinned.

"Five snails. And believe me they weren't easy to find. I had to climb a wall into a garden, one of those fabulous villas higher up, you know? I was petrified someone was going to emerge from the house and arrest me."

Beth picked up a small one that was a spiral of browns and creams. It closed up briefly, then a head emerged, antennae waving as it tried to find where the floor had gone.

"See its little eyes at the end there?"

They both peered close.

"And look at that one. It's like it's made of amber."

"They're gorgeous. I can absolutely understand why they're Pat's favourite pet, can't you?"

"She takes them with her wherever she goes."

"I know. In a bag with a lettuce."

Beth tucked the snail back under a leaf, stood and hugged Jacqui.

"Thank you. It's the best present I've ever had."

Jacqui laughed, hugged her back.

"I doubt that."

"It's true. Really it is. They never gave me gifts, he said he had more important things to spend his money on."

Jacqui had brought back a bottle of *prosecco* too.

"Sorry it's not chilled," she said as she expertly popped the cork, filled two chunky glasses.

"To the birthday girl."

They clinked, sipped. Beth walked across to the window, stood with her back to the room staring out at nothing: mist, puddles, a folded sun umbrella down below. There was a stillness about her that disturbed Jacqui.

"Beth? What is it?"

"He did once give me something," she said quietly. "His idea of a gift anyway. Just after my twenty first birthday."

She stopped.

"Go on."

Beth took a deep breath. With a finger she traced a raindrop slithering down the glass.

"He'd been out drinking for a change – he didn't often. Who'd want to sit in a pub with him? I was sound asleep. Suddenly I woke up and found him standing over my bed. I could just about see him from the light through the half open door. He put a finger across his lips and whispered shush, then he sat on the edge of the bed, nearly fell off, stupid drunken idiot. I shuffled away, but he edged close again, leant over me and pushed a strand of my hair back off my forehead. Pretty hair, he muttered. He ran his knuckles down my cheek. His skin was like… yuk. I felt sick."

Beth sipped her drink. Sipped again.

"He said he had a birthday surprise for me, that I was a big girl now, a grown up. Then he – I've never told anyone about this, Jacqui, no-one."

She stopped. Jacqui waited.

"Then before I could get away from him he lunged, threw himself on top of me, one hand pressed against my chest, I could hardy breathe, the other between our bodies, trying to push my nightie out of the way, then he worked his way down… down between my legs, his fingers sort of scrabbling at me, he wedged one leg between mine and I couldn't stop him…"

There were footsteps in the corridor, voices, laughter, other guests heading for their room. A door banged.

"I screamed, shouted get off me you dirty old pervert. He clamped his hand over my mouth but I bit his finger. Should have heard his language. When I swung my knee up to get away from him I must have really hurt him because suddenly he doubled over. I fell out of bed, crawled to the other side of the room and started to scream and he stumbled to his feet, backed away holding up his hands, saying OK calm down, what's the matter with you? When he'd gone I slammed the door and wedged a chair under it. Can't imagine that auntie didn't hear me - she must have."

More voices passing outside their door, low and intense. Arguing probably. Then silence.

"She never mentioned it and he didn't so maybe I dreamt the whole thing. Well, nightmared the whole thing. Is there such a word?"

The glass slipped from Beth's fingers.

As it hit the tiled floor it shattered into a thousand splinters. She gave a small moan, crouched down and began to scoop them up.

"Look what I've done now," she sobbed. "I'm so stupid."

The tears were unexpected. She wasn't even sure what she was crying about. Jacqui caught her hand, tugged her to her feet.

"Leave that. We'll get a broom, do it later."

Gently she edged her towards the bed where they both sat, wrapped her arms around the heaving shoulders.

"Come on, sweetheart. You're going to make your eyes so red."

But Beth couldn't stop crying. The anger, the hurt, the humiliation, all of it, pent up for far too long, and now finally released. Though it was only early evening the room was dim, cool. They sat like that for what seemed like ages. Eventually she ran out of tears.

"Right. All done?" Jacqui said, reaching for the box of tissues.

Beth took one, then another, nodded, gave a hesitant smile.

"I've had an idea and you, my girl, are going to love it."

She lay back on the bed, plumped up the pillows, patted the space beside her. As Beth joined her she slid her arm beneath her so they snuggled close.

"We're going to take a leaf out of Pat's book."

Beth sniffed, dabbed at her eyes.

"And how do we do that?"

"It's obvious. We think of some diabolical punishment that would mean Uncle Ronald never touches anyone again, the bastard."

"You mean... we kill him?"

Beth twisted to look up at Jacqui.

"No. Far too easy. Besides, he wouldn't suffer and we want him to suffer, don't we?"

Beth rested her head back on Jacqui's soft shoulder; she could smell the lemon shampoo she'd bought yesterday, a hint of the wine they'd been drinking.

She closed her eyes but she wasn't sleepy.

"I was thinking more.... I don't know... a horrible accident?"

"In his shop then," Beth said.

Jacqui kissed her lightly on the forehead.

"Of course. Good thinking. That place must be crammed with lethal implements."

"You're not kidding. You take your life in your hands when you open the door. Knives, hammers, drills, nails, hooks. Saws. Axes. Scalpels."

"And chemicals?" Jacqui added. "Like acids, bleaches, toxic glues..."

"He's always saying I should be careful, not to touch this or that. Leave it to him. He's used to handling all the dangerous stuff, he says. Like he's so clever."

"Over confident then. Perfect. Who would have thought he'd make such a terrible mistake, and get all his fingers cut off like that? Or burnt off?"

"Or trapped. When no-one was around to hear him shout for help."

"It must have been agony."

Beth was enjoying this. They both were.

"Hard to believe it happened, but then accidents do, all the time."

"He wasn't concentrating."

"Probably ogling some girl through the window."

"Sad but ...

Beth turned onto her back and sighed.

"I couldn't do it, of course."

"Sure you could. Well, with my help you could."

Beth closed her eyes, opened them again to meet Jacqui's steady gaze.

"Really? You'd do that for me?"

Jacqui hesitated then leant forwards and touched her lips very gently to Beth's.

Slowly, slowly.

Beth pulled back briefly but then stayed perfectly still as Jacqui kissed her again, this time letting her lips linger, moving them ever so slightly, opening her mouth a fraction. Did she imagine it or did Beth's lips soften beneath hers, as though yielding, as though she too was enjoying the kiss?

Then Jacqui sat up abruptly.

"Of course I would. As soon as we get back home. I promise."

She gazed out of the window.

"Looks like the rain's clearing. Come on, let's tart ourselves up and go and celebrate your birthday in style."

"And we can make plans while we eat."

"We certainly can."

And so it began.

DROUGHT

The American claimed to have been watering his garden with *acqua minerale*, though it was hard to believe, the price of it, lorries having to bring the precious water down from the north of Italy. There was talk of one being hijacked, its contents making millions of lire on the black market. Still, though, he was certainly doing something. His garden remained an oasis, green and lush, statues of naked cherubs made modest by giant maidenhair ferns, philodendrons, pastel roses twirled up limbs and around necks.

Elsewhere young plants died, too tender to survive, some shrivelling overnight. People too wilted beneath a sky that had been that same shocking blue for months now, the temperature climbing as summer filled the narrow village streets with tourists from abroad, with Italians from Bologna, Rome, Naples. Showers in hotels were limited to certain hours, and then were little more than a trickle; toilets frequently failed to flush at all.

If it was hard on the visitors, it was worse for those who lived and worked there, the cooks and bank assistants and cleaners, their days devoted to ensuring the visitors a good time. The locals who lived not in the centre, but up above the village, climbing steps under a night sky powdered with stars, the air still oven-hot, sweat running down their backs. To try to sleep for a few hours before heading back down to work.

It was during this summer, the driest for nearly twenty years, that it happened, the thing with the countess.

She may not have been a real countess, no-one knew for sure. But you could tell she was someone special, a woman of breeding, used to gracious living: Waterford glasses for her wine, aromatic oils for her bath, an Irish baroque stool made of walnut for when her feet ached. Though elderly now she still drew glances, admiration even, as she went quietly about her business dressed in white, always in white, lace at her neck and wrists, a white parasol sheltering her from the sun. Her skin was pale with golden freckles.

They invented a past for her, told of a night flight on foot across the snowy wastes of Russia or Romania, a husband dead of broken pride or kidnapped or worse. Like many who live simple lives, their imagination made up for what their days lacked.

No-one knew the truth. They didn't want to, fearing disappointment. They knew only that she'd arrived with sufficient money to buy outright the small pink and yellow villa on the edge of the village, its shutters opening out on a view of the sea, the small grey beach where fishermen worked at their nets; where in high summer a wave of sunseekers sprawled, drank warm *peroni*, played ball games. And that she lived somewhere in the north, came back to the village in the spring, stayed until the nights grew long and dark figs hung heavy from trees. That one day the villa doors would be locked, the place empty, but always, the following year, she would return.

You wouldn't have thought she would have much in common with him. Anything, come to that.

He, after all, was young, strong, wild. *Pazzo*, the locals called him, touching a finger to their foreheads. Crazy. If he wasn't eating or sleeping he was fighting. His scars told tales of jealousy, revenge, of springtime lustings. He was unpredictable; the villagers walked wide around him.

And then, one evening in June, he was waiting by her door, just sitting there. As though it was the normal thing. As though expected.

"Hello."

She hesitated, then smiled. She spoke in English though she knew many languages, spoke each one with the same precision as when she dressed, applied rouge, a whisper of blue eyeshadow. Or peeled *nespole*, a local fruit that tasted of plums and peaches, her favourite; she was carrying some now. Inside were stones that could have been made of wood. She'd planted some in pots but they hadn't taken.

He stood, stretched, yawned. There was a gash on his head, blood tracing the lines across his broad forehead. As he moved she noticed a limp.

"What have you done? Fighting, I bet. Better come inside."

Whilst she fumbled for her key, pushed aside the heavy door, he stood patiently. Then, wagging his tail, he padded obediently behind her.

In the bathroom, on the white tiled floor, the dog sat motionless whilst the countess washed his wounds. Carefully her knotted hands felt along his leg, examined his paw, his thick blunt claws. Nothing seemed broken, there were no cuts, no thorns to be plucked. Probably a pulled muscle.

He watched her with eyes the colour of butter. Once, his large hot tongue touched her hand.

She poured water and he lapped noisily, splashing it everywhere. Having no dog food in the house she shared her own meal with him: pasta with cheese. He ate ravenously. She found some *crostini* left over from the night before. That too disappeared in a few gulps. Afterwards he dropped like a filled sack, lay with his head across his paws. His eyes closed.

It was the first time the countess had had anyone to stay. She had no close friends, those that she'd once treasured now dead or changed into strangers by time. Her husband was only a faded memory, dying so soon after their wedding that she'd not yet had the child they both longed for. She was used to being alone.

Now though it came back to her, the joy of sharing. That night she had no need of her usual brandy to encourage sleep.

He went in the quiet of dawn, scratching to be let out, rested, his cut already knitting together. The countess made tea, added two slices of lemon, watched the sky change from white to blue. The sun burned fiercely. She stayed indoors in the cool, the high dim rooms, unwilling to remove the plate she'd put down for him, its willow pattern licked spotless, to brush his coarse hair from the oriental carpet. Afraid to go out. In case. Feeling foolish she muttered a small prayer to a God she'd almost forgotten.

That evening, when he returned, she thanked God.

"I'll call you, let's see. Buster Keaton, for your sad face. What do you think?"

The dog looked away, sighed, then his eyes met hers and his tail flickered. How can people say you haven't got a soul? she asked silently.

It was the start of a summer unlike any other, for both of them. Of days that stretched like elastic as they filled each hour with doing things, or doing nothing, simply sitting on the *terrazza* enjoying each other's company. Sometimes the countess read: Balzac, Dickens, the classics she'd loved in her youth but had put aside in later years, too busy, too distracted, too sad to concentrate. Now she re-discovered them, often reading aloud to the dog at her feet.

They took walks along the beach early morning and late evenings when few people were about: lovers or those soon to be, boys poking at baby crabs in pools. The countess threw sticks, awkward, unable to throw them far. The dog understood, turned in flurries of soft sand and came back for them, dropping them again at her feet, inviting her to try again.

In the village people who'd never spoken to the countess before now had an excuse. At first they warned her about the dog, his violent temper, the dangers of taking him into her home, but she just thanked them politely, walked on with Buster docile at her heels. Their doubts changed to admiration. She'd done the impossible, this frail old lady. She'd tamed a lion. *E incredibile*, they agreed. Children took their courage into small, nervous hands and patted the dog tentatively, then scampered off to boast about it. Their parents admired his shining coat.

The countess knew she'd done no more than offer friendship to an outcast. Friendship, a place to sleep, food. He, in return, had brought her back to life, his arrival as refreshing as the water she gave to the plants on her *terrazza*, sprinkling them each evening from a blue watering can. True, it was mineral water, but she could afford it and the flowers needed it.

There was always a bowl of water down on the tiled floor, too.

More than a friend, the dog was the escort she never knew she'd missed, the companion she needed to feel able to go to places she'd otherwise shun: empty night streets where only cats lurked behind bins, or into the vortex of a crowd. Once she joined the audience lining the streets to cheer participants in a cross-country bike race, young men in shorts bent low over sleek slips of metal, flashes of red and yellow, everyone urging them on with shouts of *bravo*, throwing streamers. She found it exciting in a way she'd never imagined. The dog, always close by, narrowly avoided being trampled.

Another time, thirsty from the walk back from the village grocery, from carrying bags, one in each hand, she plucked up the courage to enter a bar she'd often passed but never seen inside. Its dusky interior was a shock after the white world outside. Used to being shouted at, the dog hesitated in the doorway, then followed her, only relaxing when she rested her hand on his head. As she sat drinking a Campari under a lazily spinning fan, a local whose face she knew well invited her to join him and friends in a hand of whist. She did, and won. Delighted she bought drinks for everyone, and another for herself before leaving a little unsteadily, the dog coming out from under a bench, his presence forgotten by all. Except, of course, the countess.

As summer came to a boil and the streets bubbled over with visitors, with bustle and noise, the two friends took to the hills behind the village. Here they found peace, dappled shade, the sharp green smell of pine trees; the gentle hum of insect life disturbed only by the crackling of twigs, a noise that made the countess pause, look around, lift her nose to test for a hint of smoke. Forest fires were causing destruction throughout the south. Crops were being lost as a wave of flames swept across farmland, uncontrollable, going on to more remote areas where wild goats and sheep, foxes, other creatures already weakened by the drought were too slow to escape. A shepherd died in a wooden hut. Even up above the village a fire had broken out, a beacon of flames that had lit up the night sky; a helicopter had spent most of the next day circling to collect buckets of sea water with which to douse it.

"Thank God you're safe here with me." the countess told the dog.

Only once, on a night when the moon was fat and white, did the dog go off alone. It was an instinctive thing, the pull of tides; even his devotion to the countess wasn't strong enough to hold him back. He returned three days later, his coat prickly with burrs, smelling of caves and bats and wild herbs. The countess put down food for him, brushed his coat. She said nothing. Her touch told him of her fears, also of her forgiveness.

And still there was no rain.

A Sirocco wind sprung up, covering the village in a fine red dust. Dust from Africa. Someone had written on a car bonnet *sono sporco, lavarmi*. All the cars were dirty, all needed to be washed, polished. But there was little enough water for necessities; using it for such luxuries was not just frowned upon, it was forbidden.

There were rumours that even the American's garden was no longer looking its best; that he'd cancelled the party he held each year for his wife's birthday so that no-one would see it.

One evening lightning flashed out over the sea, serrating the black silk sky, thunder rumbled half-heartedly. The storm, though, never reached land, but was lost somewhere at sea. The tourists, wanting only sun for their tans, smiled with relief; locals muttered their disappointment.

For the countess, the problem of obtaining enough water was minor compared with something far more worrying. As autumn touched the sparse trees and shrubs, and even the air seemed to be tinted with gold, she knew soon she must leave. And what, then, would happen to Buster?

He couldn't go with her, she knew that; wouldn't be happy caged in a flat in a grey northern city. He'd go berserk. Yet if she left him behind he may well be run out of the village, would die of starvation. Or he could be rounded up with the other strays and destroyed. She didn't know which was worse. Sleep was impossible; she'd get up in the early hours, slipping on a housecoat, pad along to the kitchen to make tea. The sleeping dog would stir, lift his head, then follow her out onto the *terrazza* as though on an invisible cord.

He knew. He knew that something was wrong, was more reluctant than ever to leave the countess's side. He was forever touching her, resting his head on her knees or her feet, nuzzling her empty hand, demanding the reassurance of contact. She even thought, though could have been imagining it, that he seemed reluctant to close his eyes.

There was one option, not a good one, but she had to do something.

Her mind was made up. She plucked up courage, knocked at the door of neighbours who lived there all year round, a small house further down the hill that had a pram outside, an old Vespa the husband used to go to work somewhere along the coast. They could almost certainly use some extra money, especially during the winter.

A young woman answered, one baby on her hip, another clinging to the hem of her dress.

"*Mi scusi, ma voglio domandare un favore.*"

She took a deep breath.

"Could you possibly take in my dog for the winter? I mean.... look after him? I'll pay, of course, for his food and also your help."

The young woman looked down at the dog, quiet now certainly, but big, muscular. She knew about him, knew of his reputation. She had children to consider; besides, she didn't much care for animals in the house. They brought in fleas. She shrugged apologetically.

"*Mi dispiace. Non e possibile.*"

"How much would you need? I can be generous. Please at least..."

For a brief second the countess hated Buster for making her beg when never in her life had she begged anyone to do anything. For making her vulnerable, needy.

But still the woman shook her head. Her husband would be furious if she agreed to such a thing; would say she had no right, that she was a bad mother.

The baby sneezed then started to wail. The countess turned away.

She asked others. More excuses were made, some genuine, some obviously not. The answer was the same: no, sorry. Eventually, though, an elderly man approached her on the street, unshaven, his breath smelling of beer. A drunk, she decided. But there was something about him: he had kind eyes. And before he spoke he reached out and touched the dog's head lightly but confidently. Tugged at the thick soft ears.

"I can look after your dog for you," he said. "If you pay me. You can trust me, I like dogs."

He'd probably only give Buster scraps, but that was something. That and a roof over his head. She had an idea. She would pay him a bonus when she returned in the spring, a generous one. If the dog had been well cared for. The man laughed, showing stained teeth. He leaned forward, put his hand on her arm, his touch hot.

"He'll be here when you return, fat and healthy. *Promesso.*"

Could she trust him? She had no choice.

That night it rained, not much, hardly more than a shower, but suddenly the air tasted fresh and sweet. The summer was over. The countess was always sad to leave, but most years she also felt a tingle of excitement at returning to the city, to her other life.

Now though her heart sank.

She remembered the man's promise as she began packing suitcases, neatly arranging the few things she brought back and forth each year, windows flung wide, the rattle of cicadas blending with the rustle of leaves on trees so that it was hard to tell which was which.

Remembered, and took some small comfort from it.

But Buster, sensing that things were changing, became increasingly disturbed. His appetite waned. He fretted to go out, then when the door was held open for him, changed his mind as though afraid she might disappear when his back was turned. His eyes spoke of betrayal.

The day before the countess was due to leave Buster lapped at his water bowl, sniffed the morning air and padded quietly outside.

He didn't come back.

She knew it was hopeless, but still the countess had to find him, had to at least try. Bent now by worry she trudged the streets, climbed the never-ending steps, crossed tiny *piazzas* where boys still in school uniform threw stones at pigeons; she'd have liked to scold them but there was no time. She forgot her parasol and grew red in the face, her feet sore, stopping frequently now, hand pressed to her chest.

The word was passed on, the locals surprised and dismayed. Their concern was not for the dog; dogs were a nuisance, they messed everywhere, frightened children, they could be dangerous, even carry rabies. But because of this dog they'd come to know and like the countess who had lived in their midst as a stranger, for so many years. She was important to them; the dog was important to her; hence they were concerned.

The countess delayed her departure.

Whilst tourists piled into cars, or took taxis to the airport, and hotels grew empty, were cleaned for a final time, shuttered, the countess sat and waited. Time and again she sensed the dog at the door, heard him snuffling, hurried to open it, her heart pounding, only to find it was the wind trying to get in. Her imagination. Ghosts.

She forgot to put on make-up; her white skirt was marked with dust and yet not washed. Forgetting to eat she grew thinner, her face seeming to suddenly collapse like the last few sandcastles on the beach. She felt tired. She felt old.

Stories reached her. A dog dead by the side of the *autostrada* above the village, hit probably by a truck, so badly mangled it was hard to say if it was Buster; but no, the man who brought the news was fairly sure it was a different dog. He was sure, in fact. A chicken farm up in the mountains had been raided by a large brown animal; the *contadino* thought it more likely to be a dog than a fox. He had shot at him but missed. Someone thought he'd seen Buster in a pack of dogs that was running wild in a village further along the coast, killing cats and making the streets unsafe at night so that a committee was being formed, plans made to use poison, or guns, or both. She couldn't bare to think about such things. Besides, none of the sightings could be Buster. The countess knew, deep inside. It wasn't possible.

Or was it? Could he have reverted to the wild creature he was before her love had tamed him? Everything was her fault. She'd made him trust her then she'd let him down. She'd driven him away.

The countess couldn't sleep. She rose from her bed, went out onto the *terrazza* and stood watching the drama as lightning flashed on and off illuminating the village below, making everything look unreal, like a stage setting. Suddenly she realised it was raining, gentle at first, then heavy, a torrent, water splashing off the tiled floor, a sound she had almost forgotten. She was soaked through in minutes.

By lunchtime next day the villa was locked, empty except for a hopeful mouse who searched the kitchen and found nothing, not even crumbs. As usual, the countess had swept round carefully before leaving.

The following spring new people were seen to have taken over the villa: a young couple, yellow haired, Scandinavian possibly, with three long-legged children. There were shouts, laughter, music playing from a radio. Parties on the *terrazza* where women in backless dresses drank *negronis* from long glasses and compared birth signs whilst their men compared careers, admired each other's wives. Bikinis and trunks dried on the line. The only time crying was heard was when one of the children fell, or awoke in the middle of the night from a bad dream.

WHATEVER MAKES YOU HAPPY

A wasp had fallen into the *cappuccino* the waiter had brought to her table just moments before, clunking it down as his eyes followed a girl in a bikini on a scooter. Or the wasp had deliberately dived into it. Louise thought it might have been a suicide attempt, the brief pause above the cup, the sudden plummeting. No wasp was going to leave her with that on her conscience. She scooped it out with a spoon, tipped it onto the table where it staggered about for a bit as though drunk, then set about cleaning its legs, one at a time. Maybe it just liked the taste of coffee?

Satisfied, it lifted up into the air like a helicopter, hovered and then was gone. Louise smiled to herself. It was a good sign: it meant that Antonio would come.

Or – probably better still – it might mean he'd changed his mind and wasn't coming.

But of course he would. He would be there soon, a few minutes late but not hurrying. Men of the *mezzogiorno* never hurried. He would smile – the nearest thing to an apology – before he reached the table, would scrape back a chair and then sit without a word; his eyes would seek hers. She had met him only yesterday at the opening of a hand dyed batik exhibition: swirling fish and insect designs in vibrant blues and greens hanging from cord lines stretched across the room. It was part of her job to be there. He'd been invited by the batik artist who was a friend of many years.

Not that they'd talked about much. From the moment they'd been introduced she'd felt the attraction, had stood close so she could hear when he did speak, had smiled so much she was beginning to feel embarrassed. And then they were broken apart by the bustling crowds, by the need to talk to other people.

Just as she was about to leave he'd appeared at her side.

"Louise. Is OK to call you Louise?" His voice had been dark and smooth. She thought he could have been an opera singer with a voice like that, though he was too tall and slim, angular even. An actor then, a stage actor.

"Please, I hope you don't mind my asking, but I'd be very happy if you would lunch with me tomorrow. I would cook for myself anyway, something simple. *Spaghetti alle vongole* possibly. You're not too shy to enjoy eating spaghetti, are you?"

He smiled to show he was teasing. Or challenging her? Nice teeth, very white, just a glint of a gold filling on the right. You couldn't call him handsome, but attractive, definitely. So he was inviting her to his home. They hardly knew each other. He had a confidence that was bordering on arrogance. But only just.

"I have also some Lacryma Christi del Vesuvio Rosato, the wine you talked about, yes?" he added, as though that would convince her.

Earlier, over the cocktails and canapes, a small group had been discussing wines. It was agreed that one of the best was a local wine made from grapes grown near Naples, a special variety found nowhere else in Italy. The wine had the fragrance of oranges blossom; it glowed delicately.

Louise had admitted she'd never tried it.

Everyone had expressed surprise. So he'd remembered.

They were standing in the way; people pushed past them heading home or more likely out for the evening. No-one seemed to sleep at night here, it was too hot.

"Fine," she'd said then. "I'd like that."

Having tried to explain how to find his house, he'd given up. The village streets and steps and piazzas were as complex as a crossword puzzle. He would meet her at the bar, they agreed. At twelve. Then he was gone, back to join the last few guests still chatting amongst the batik sheets.

She was early on purpose, liked sitting under a giant blue umbrella watching people pass. Watching open-top cars, scooters, and once, five boys on skates twisting through them, as quick and sure as snakes. Watching cats sitting motionless under tables, eyes focused for birds. There were more birds around than last time she was here; finches and sparrows, a couple she didn't recognise. Strange how at home she hardly noticed the birds, wasn't really interested, yet here they gave her so much pleasure.

It was always like that, being here; as though she'd stepped out of her everyday world, her real life, and was floating free, seeing things with sharper eyes, ears picking up inaudible sounds. Even the air on her skin felt different.

The coffee was lukewarm. Why had she ordered it anyway? She fancied something cold and alcoholic: an aperol spritz, lots of ice and bubbles. The waiter came at once, the tables around her were quiet, most visitors still on the beach burning themselves to a frazzle. He left the bill on the table and she called him back, paid him at once. She needed to get that done, didn't want Antonio to think he had to pay for her. She already felt guilty enough.

Antonio.

It was obvious what would happen. She could see it all.

He would push back the wrought-iron gate, welcome her to his house – his weekend house, he would explain. He lectured in Naples during the week, came here to escape car fumes, the telephone, the necessity to accompany his wife to dinner parties or the theatre or shopping. She, his nameless wife, felt insecure away from the city, preferred to stay in their elegant Vomera apartment that - even though it was high above the city - he found stifling in the summer. Though she joined him occasionally; when they had family from the north visiting, and in August of course. Only tourists and the very poor stayed in the city in August.

Your wife is happy for you to be here alone? she'd want to ask, but wouldn't. Such arrangements were common in this part of the world. Maybe his wife was also happy to be alone sometimes.

Louise knew all there was to know about arrangements: how easy they were to set up, how they were the perfect compromise that meant everyone would be satisfied. No more tears, no tantrums, no hurt feelings. Certainly no jealousy. She also knew life was never that simple.

He would pause to look at what he called his *giardino*, though to her it was a cluster of pots with some parched plants rather than a garden. If he could find one he'd pick a flower – a rose or poppy – and give it to her. She would say something silly to show she was unimpressed by such romantic gestures, would discard the flower as she followed him up a flight of white stone steps into the house.

A dark wooden table would be set for lunch with a knobbly lace tablecloth – made no doubt by his grandmother – and tall fragile glasses, heavy cutlery. From a tiny kitchen to the right would drift the smell of tomato sauce, torn basil leaves.

"Come." He would beckon her to the window. She had dressed casually: a soft cheesecloth blouse in a pale peach colour, a white cotton skirt, her long pale hair tied at the back of her neck though wisps always escaped. She would slip off her white espadrilles to show she was at home, walk towards him feeling aware of her body inside her clothes. Her toes would curl against the cold of the floor.

Beyond would be a stunning view of cliffs, beach, sea stretching out and up to blend with the sky, a vast blue canvas.

She would notice instead his after shave, or more likely his cologne. Expensive, carefully chosen by him. His shirt would be very white; would he have washed and ironed it himself? Or would his wife have done it? She had her own work, he'd say, and Louise would agree about that being important. She too had a job: represented a company that imported fashion from India, floaty ethnic dresses that were the trend these days, was here to persuade the boutiques to stock them alongside the distinctive locally made clothes, to convince them of the increased profits. His wife wouldn't need to work, not financially, but neither did she.

He'd use a laundry service of course.

The wine, when poured from the misted bottle, sparkled with promise.

"Smell it first," he would say, holding his own glass close to his face, breathing deeply. She would close her eyes, copy him, and be whisked back to her childhood, summer holidays in Cornwall, to hedges bursting with blossom of all kinds.

"Now. Sip slowly."

The wine would be all that she expected.

Over lunch they would talk, flirt. And when he passed her something – the bowl of *arugula* salad, the pepper mill – or when he topped up her glass, he would make sure his fingers did not touch hers, not even the lightest brush. Which she would find more exciting than if they had.

A traffic hold up in the narrow road in front of the bar brought her back to the present. A lorry delivering ice cream had parked in such a way that nothing – except a scooter with a man, woman and two small children curved together like spoons – could pass. There was bibbing of horns, shouting, hand gestures that anyone could understand. But not for the first time Louise noticed that no-one seemed truly angry. It was like a game to them, a drama everyone could join in with, could enjoy. And then the driver hurried out, jumped into the cab and zoomed off followed by a stream of vehicles. Someone applauded.

Was it the climate that made people here so much more relaxed, so ready to make the most of each moment? She envied them; she took things far too seriously. She analysed. She anticipated problems, disasters. Taking risks was meant to be exciting but for her...

Then again, she'd married Terry, hadn't she? Everyone had said that was a risky thing to do.

"But he's so much older than you, what, twenty years?"

"He's always travelling, and not to nice safe places. They don't even have road in some of those third world countries."

"And the crime is horrific, people getting mugged, their throats cut for just a few coins."

She hadn't listened, hadn't cared, knew only that with him she felt complete. Still felt that way. So why was she here, waiting for a man she didn't know called Antonio?

When – after lunch – it came to coffee on the *terrazzo,* the village lying torpid from too much food and drink and heat, that was when she should say thank you, it was lovely, I must go now.

Or, she had the choice.

She could follow him down more stairs to a bedroom, the shutters drawn, the bed covered with a rose damask bedspread – his wife's choice? - its tassels brushing the floor. On the wall above it would be the crucifix that was to be found everywhere in this Catholic country, as much part of the décor as a clock.

She could let him remove her clothes, gently, tenderly, as though she were a child. Shivering now she would turn away as he removed his.

Could lie with him on the bed and make love. And remember what it felt like to be desired, to be held by muscular arms, to be kissed gently, passionately. To be a woman. Though she never admitted it to herself – it was too dangerous, too sad – Louise longed for that. Just sometimes she really longed for it.

"Do whatever makes you happy Louise," Terry had said time and again. "For my sake."

He'd given her that look that had broken her heart.

"Please. Will you?"

She understood what he was saying. That she was young still, and that he was a shattered ruin of a man who couldn't walk, couldn't even stand.

"I mean it. I want it. Just promise me you'll always come back to me."

She'd take his hand, his fine fingers always cold these days, press them to her face. But then she'd change the subject.

Ironic that it had been a car accident on a quiet country road that had shattered his body, and both their lives. Not his age, which in fact was nineteen years more than hers. Not his journeying to far flung places to organise clean water for people who had to walk miles for their supply. Drunken teenagers who were driving like maniacs had smashed into Terry's Volvo as he drove steadily home - within the speed limit of course - from a late meeting, rolling it down a bank to come to a halt against an especially beautiful old oak tree. Afterwards, he'd repeatedly worried that it might have been damaged.

Louise had been convinced she was going to lose him for the first few weeks. When he grew stronger she was over the moon, didn't care that he was going to be in a wheelchair for the rest of his life. She had him back and that was all that mattered. Her Terry. Her life.

And now, here she was preparing to go to bed with a total stranger because Terry had asked her to, not in so many words but that was what he meant. If she did, she'd enjoy it, she knew that, Antonio would ensure she did. Making a woman happy in bed was a matter of pride to men like him, experienced lovers who knew the subtle, tantalising, sometimes shocking things to do to a woman's body to give her pleasure.

It wouldn't mean anything of course. She might see him again, once or twice during the few days she was based in the village, and then it would be over. And forgotten. Or maybe she'd suffer a little, remember what she was missing, maybe she'd want more. And if she met someone else, someone she felt attracted to...well, Terry would be fine with that. Maybe he'd even be happy, thinking that this arrangement meant she'd never need to leave him.

She understood, but still it felt strange. Wrong.

Exciting too of course.

The sun had moved around and Louise shuffled her chair into the shade of the umbrella and away from the burning heat. A big black flying bug hovered near her and she flapped it gently away, unsure if it was likely to sting or not. She still hadn't got used to the size of the things. And what was it with her and insects today?

She took another sip of her drink, the ice now melted.

She checked her watch; it was midday. People were ambling up from the beach for lunch, some stopping for a beer or *granita di limone,* sea-wet towels draped on the back of chairs, sandy feet nudging each other under the table.

There was still time; she could simply scoop up her bag and go. She could escape and not have to make any more decisions.

Or she could stay and let whatever was going to happen, happen.

*

Antonio arrived nine minutes late, ran an eye over the tables searching for Louise. One table, at the far end, was unoccupied, though on it there was an empty glass, beside it a heavy ceramic ashtray under which he could see a paper napkin. Without hesitating he walked across to it, picked up the napkin and unfolded it.

There was just one word. SORRY.

He smiled, shrugged, then dropped into the chair Louise had just vacated, beckoned to the waiter and ordered a whisky sour.

LEARNING TO SWIM

Almost.

He was almost there.

Charlie held his breath as he tip-toed bare footed across the cold tiled floor, past the ornate, cluttered reception desk – no-one behind it this time of day of course - and eased the heavy wooden door open. It made a tiny sound, no more than a squeak, but still his heart stopped. Someone would hear. He waited, but no-one emerged from behind the thick blue curtain that led to the back rooms, the kitchen, the private area that belonged to the *pensione* owners. They were up already; he'd heard voices as he edged down the stairs and into the hall, the two girls who mum said were the daughters and far too young to be working, silly creatures, always tittering. He couldn't stand them. They were too busy gossiping now to notice him.

He swung the door open, stepped outside into a hushed world, the air moist and heavy after last night's storm. The ground was wet and steaming. Charlie took a deep breath, then tugged one sandal out of each pocket of his shorts, slipped them on.

He wanted to cheer.

He'd done it, escaped. They were still in bed and sound asleep, mum and Ted, Mr Know It All, Mr Smart Arse. They'd been at it again last night. They must realise he could hear them, his little box room was only the other side of the wall, his bed right up against it, mum gasping, ooh Ted, that's so good, yes there, touch me there, and Ted grunting like a pig, and then she'd scream like he was doing something terrible to her, then suddenly go quiet. Charlie had gone out into the hall and tentatively opened their door a crack so he could watch them, but they had the shutters closed and the room was dim, and besides, he couldn't see much from that angle. Then Ted walked past, stark naked, skinny and white except for his sunburnt arms and shoulders.

The ginger cat sidled over to Charlie, optimistic and yet also ready to be kicked. He bent and stroked her dry hard head and she pushed up against his palm, twisted around his ankles. Nothing of her, but she had nipples underneath. Pregnant, mum said. Probably all be born dead, or they'll die soon anyway. These street cats are randy little buggers. They're all flea ridden, probably got rabies too. Don't touch it, Charlie. Promise me you won't, OK? He'd promised.

"Nothing for you today," he whispered, crouching down so she could nudge his outstretched fingers. "Sorry."

The last two days he'd sneaked out some bits he'd saved from snacks they'd had during the day, cheese, that ham stuff with the funny name, a couple of squares of pasta with something in them, he'd no idea what but she scoffed them anyway. They snacked all the time, that was why mum was so fat. She was always on a diet but here, on holiday, well, you have to relax and give yourself a treat sometimes, don't you? Seemed to Charlie she was always giving herself treats.

"Later. I'll get you something, promise."

He was anxious to get going, just in case someone had heard him and he got hauled back. They didn't want him to bother them, but they didn't want him out of sight either. He wished he'd never come but Ted was insistent.

"Bring the lad along, it'll be good for him, see a bit of the world. Not been to Italy, has he?"

"Not been anywhere," his mum had replied in that whinging voice she put on when she wanted pity. She'd reached to push

Charlie's hair from his forehead and he'd shaken her off, shuffled away.

"His dad took him to Blackpool once. Lost him, he did, Can you imagine? Too busy with some bird he'd picked up."

"He didn't feel well," Charlie had said.

"And why was that?" she'd snapped back. "Nothing to do with all those beers he'd..."

"He wasn't drunk. He wasn't."

Nothing dad had done had been right for her. Except dying. Better still, it was a stupid accident at the office which should never have happened – crushed by a coffee machine he'd been helping to carry down stairs - and she'd claimed compensation and won. It wasn't much - a bloody insult she'd called it - but it had meant a new car and a huge telly, and she'd bought herself dresses and shoes and a crocodile bag, and had her hair frizzed and bleached so that she looked like Madonna. To get back my confidence, she'd said. To make me feel like a woman again.

And now she'd got herself involved with Ted who was a nightmare.

The sky was grey like it always was at home, the mountains up above the village swathed in cloud, but it was hot, as though the oven door had been left open. Charlie started down the steps leading to the beach, stones worn to a shine by other feet, the first narrow flight going between houses, high walls on either side. Suddenly he was out on the twisting road that led from the top of the village all the way down, stood back as one of the little three-wheeler trucks that were everywhere purred past. He jogged across the front of a swish hotel, all plate glass and mosaic tiles, then turned down another flight of steps. He liked the steps best, no-one would see him, though to be honest there were few people around anyway. It was great. Just how he'd hoped it would be. Not like during the day when there were swarms of people everywhere, on the road, on the steps, cars beeping on every corner, motor scooters ridden by youngsters wearing dark glasses zigzagging through the chaos. It was a miracle they didn't kill someone. That was what Ted said. He said they were lethal and the yobs driving them should be thrashed.

Ted was tough. He was always saying it.

"You gotta be tough if you're going to survive in this shitty world."

Mum said Ted was right.

He'd been in Hyde Park when the IRA blew up those cavalry men, hardly more than kids some of them, and their horses too. Blood and guts all over the place, the horses whinnying, hooves scrabbling on the stones as they tried to stand despite having a leg hanging off, or being full of nails. Ted had been driving a few streets away, heard the explosion and went running to help. Not that he could do anything. The police were there in no time, putting up barriers, shunting people back. A little girl, her yellow flowered dress splattered with blood, was crying so violently he'd worried that she'd asphyxiate.

"Bastards," he'd said. Mum had put her finger across her lips, glanced at Charlie to say don't go on. But later Ted had told him more about the horrors he'd seen, or read about, or one of his mates had told him about. Minor pub disagreements that turned nasty, druggies with knives too high on something to know what they were doing. More bombings.

"You've got to be able to look after yourself, Charlie boy."

He wanted him to take classes: judo, karate.

"Aikido's good. It's Japanese. What d'you think? Bet you've never heard of it."

"Course I have."

"Or some kind of sport at least. Running, long jump, anything to build stamina. Then you wouldn't have to pretend to be sick on school sports day."

Why couldn't he at least try to understand? It was Charlie's first year at the comprehensive, miles from his last school, he didn't know anyone, not a single familiar face and he'd never found it easy to make friends. He was struggling to fit in.

"I didn't pretend."

Even to him that sounded weak.

"I didn't." Stronger this time.

Mum said he shouldn't keep answering Ted back, but he couldn't help it. Ted was always on at him, always poking him to get a reaction, like he had that dead squirrel that was outside their front door for days. Eventually it was gone, just a clump of tatty brown fur left to mark the spot.

And then, somehow, he'd discovered Charlie's secret.

"You can't swim? Go on. You're kidding. Nearly in your teens and you can't swim?"

He'd made it sound like Charlie was bed wetting or something awful like that. So he couldn't swim. Not surprising when they lived in the middle of a big city, the only swimming pool the council one where noise bounced off the walls, with its smell of chlorine, and pee in the showers where boys had competitions to see who could pee up the walls the highest. He knew, he'd seen them.

"Tell you what. I'll teach you."

Oh no. No, no.

"In Italy. We'll have a whole week with a hotel pool on our doorstep."

Already Charlie had been reluctant to go on this holiday, even though it meant missing school which was of course a plus. Now he was dreading it.

"I tell you, by the time we come home you'll be swimming like …"

"I won't." Charlie said. "I can't, my feet don't work properly."

Ted had chuckled.

"They will, Believe me, they will."

Charlie thought about the swimming trunks mum had got for him, two pairs, one pair yellow with bright blue trims, the others a green and purple pattern. You couldn't miss them from a mile away; he might as well have come out wearing a pineapple on his head. Right now they were on a chair on the balcony, though they'd be wet again with the rain. He imagined putting them on, how they'd cling to him. He shuddered. He imagined another lesson at the pool, Ted trying to stay calm and encouraging. Come on, you can do it. Arms straight, chin on the water, now kick hard. Your feet are fine, they'll hold you up, just kick. Let go of the side, Charlie, you're not going to learn if… oh for Christ's sake.

As he stomped off to get a drink - boy, did he need one, he muttered - Charlie heard him add the words he knew he'd hear sooner or later.

"Best thing to do? Chuck him in. He'll learn quickly enough then."

There was no swimming lesson the next day.

They'd gone on a trip, packed into a hot coach with windows that wouldn't open, fat people spilling out of their seats, a baby screaming. As the guide pointed up to Vesuvius – a giant bowl gently steaming – Charlie had prayed that it would erupt suddenly and hurl them all into the sea below. Mum had loved

Sorrento, so many shops full of trinkets and souvenirs and little bottles of yellow and blue liquors. Ted of course had preferred Pompeii, especially the plaster casts of bodies of the people who'd died there two thousand years ago, thrashing about, suffocated, buried alive by hot ash. Mum had thought it gruesome.

Charlie didn't care about any of it. He just wanted to be somewhere else.

Now he stopped by a low wall fringed with greenery, flowers like white stars: for a moment he was distracted by a flicker of gold as a lizard the size of his little finger scampered along the top and then plummeted over the edge. The sea was greyer than usual, but soft and smooth. He'd decided: he going down to the beach. He didn't know why, or what he'd do when he got there, but escaping was no good if you didn't have a purpose. Something to run TO as well as FROM.

He'd think of a plan when he got there.

"*Buon giorno.*" An old woman in black, on her way up the steps with a cardboard box full of what looked like vegetables balanced on her head, nodded as they passed. Charlie looked at his feet and muttered.

Another road to be crossed. More steps going down, these ones wider, many of them lined with plastic bags fat with rubbish. A couple had been torn open; bloody cats again, mum would have said. He was getting into the rhythm now, moving steadily, lightly from step to step. He even began a gentle jog, enjoying the movement, the feeling of freedom.

And then he was there. The final flight of steps stopped and he found himself on a wide paved promenade, sand in the cracks, shops and cafes on one side, most of them still closed. On the other side were a few tired looking palm trees. And beyond them, the beach. He'd seen the beach from the streets up above, knew that come midday it would be packed with people. Already the rows of beach chairs were being tidied up to make neat rows, red umbrellas were slotted into heavy bases and opened. It was like being in an empty room before the party started.

Charlie hesitated, then looked to the right. Far along there was what looked like a small quay, a single boat attached to the rock, blue and white though it had seen better days. A skinny and very tanned young man in shorts and T-shirt was taking boxes from a pile on the quay, transferring them one by one to the boat. Charlie ambled over, stood watching. The man glanced up, squinting against the sky which was gradually brightening, patches of blue here and there, the sun now only lightly veiled.

"*Ciao,*" he said. "*Puoi aiutarmi*?

Charlie shrugged.

"I don't speak Italian."

The man nodded, then waved a hand at the boxes and beckoned, and Charlie understood he wanted him to pass one over. Delighted to help he hurried forward. It was heavier than he'd expected, contained cans of beer, as did the next one. Another box had crisps, and another seemed to be full of tomatoes.

Charlie was disappointed when they'd all been packed. He stood looking out to sea, trying to tell exactly where the water became sky.

"You English?" the man said. Charlie nodded. "Good. I speak." He held up a hand, thumb and finger curled to leave a tiny gap between them. "*Un po'*. A little."

He turned away, then stopped.

"You want come?" he said.

Charlie hesitated. Of course he did. But.

"To beach."

He pointed along the coast and Charlie could just make out a wedge of grey sand nestling at the foot of the craggy cliffs, what looked like a small hut, some red umbrellas.

"I leave this for the bar, come back. Yes?"

Charlie knew he should say no, the man was a stranger. He imagined mum and Ted waking up, knocking on his door, finding him gone. Maybe mum would panic – she often did, for no reason at all – then decide he'd gone down for breakfast. He thought about breakfast at home: cornflakes and a splash of going-off milk usually, eaten with dread because soon he'd be on his way to school. He thought about Ted being furious when he realised Charlie really wasn't there anymore. That he'd escaped.

He didn't hesitate.

"Yes please," he said, bending and dropping awkwardly into the boat which rocked gently then settled.

"*Bene. Sono Marco.*" The man held out his hand which was hot, dry, his long fingers curling around Charlie's.

"You are?"

"Charlie."

Another quick nod, then Marco clambered over the boxes to the rear of the boat and started the engine which made Charlie think of the lawn mower his dad used to use. It chugged. Surely it wasn't powerful enough to get them there and back?

Slowly the boat moved away from the quay heading straight out towards the horizon. Was that right? Charlie, erect on the wooden seat, realised he'd stopped breathing. Suddenly he felt very small and fragile, a tiny dot on a vast and dangerous ocean.

But gradually the gliding movement of the boat calmed him and he began to breathe again. And then, to enjoy himself. They were still heading away from land and he could start to worry, if he chose. But when the man asked if he was OK, he knew he was being treated to this extra ride, this adventure. As a thank you for his help maybe. Or maybe the man just wanted an excuse for some time out before having to unpack all those boxes at the beach.

Suddenly Marco stood, squinting out towards the ocean as though trying hard to see something, then bent and shut off the engine. In the silence the boat seemed to shudder, then settled. He pointed.

"*Guarda*. You see?"

Charlie stood up too, held onto the side of the boat to steady himself. He'd no idea what he was meant to be looking at, all he could see was an unending expanse of flat water.

"What...?"

"Wait. You see."

The silence around them was something he felt he could touch, like a blanket, but then in the far distance he heard the first bus of the day snaking along the main road way up above the village, its horn beeping, echoing in the mountains above, beeping again. Then it faded.

The sea now was turning to blue as the clouds cleared.

And then he saw it, the briefest quickest movement, a flicker of life that curved up out of the water and dropped back down again. A pause, and he saw it again. Charlie's heart started to race.

"What is it?" he said. He had no idea. Some kind of giant fish, or a shark? A killer whale?

In a flash he realised that Marco knew. He'd been looking out for it, of course. That was why they were there.

"*Un delfino.*"

Charlie didn't understand. He wanted to turn to Marco but didn't dare take his eyes off the circling creature.

"*Aspetta.* I think you call it... dolphin?"

The dolphin was coming closer.

"It smiles," Marco said, pulling his own face into a wide grin to show what he meant. For a moment Charlie felt a lurch of disappointment as the dolphin swam past them but it reappeared the other side of the boat, paused, head up out of the water as it bobbed, looking straight at them. Charlie could see a row of neat white teeth.

"*Bello, non e vero?*" Marco said. "You watch. I go sit."

He waved a cigarette in the air, balanced his way to the front of the boat, sat and hunched to light it then dangled his feet over the edge. His attention was back on the coast as he sat there, humming.

The water lapped quietly against the wooden sides of the boat. Charlie watched as the dolphin swam straight out as though leaving, disappeared, arched suddenly out of the water to slide back into it again with a splash that was more like a whisper. It's tail, just before it disappeared, made Charlie think of a butterfly. It swam in close again looking up at Charlie with shiny black eyes, as though saying, what d'you think of that then?

Charlie couldn't help himself. He clapped his hands, the sound making Marco turn to glance at him, but only briefly. Charlie had the dolphin to himself. Was he the luckiest boy in the world, or what?

He'd seen a film once, on the box, a man in goggles and flippers who'd been swimming off a coast somewhere and been approached by a family of dolphins. They'd swum around him, over him, under him, whistling and clicking, not hurting him or anything, just curious. Dolphins aren't dangerous. They won't bite your leg off. That's sharks. Isn't it? He wasn't sure. But anyone could see, this dolphin wanted to be a friend. Look at the way it circled as though inviting him to join it. Begging him. It had thousands of miles of ocean for a playground and yet it chose to stay there, so close Charlie could reach out and touch it.

There was nothing in the world he wanted to do more than play with this beautiful shiny creature, but how could he? He couldn't swim. He couldn't even do a doggy paddle. He was – what did Ted call him? – a wimp.

But then, what if...?

He could risk it. So if he drowned, he drowned. He dreaded going back to England anyway, to his sad empty life with mum who wasn't interested in him now that she had Ted. And Ted, always nagging, digging, thinking he was so clever when he wasn't; he was thick as two planks.

And school.

And Mr Stafford, the maths teacher who definitely had it in for him. He hated Mr Stafford almost as much as he hated Ted.

Charlie made up his mind, glanced at Marco who was now busy coiling a length of rope.

He could do it, he knew he could.

Lifting his feet up over the side of the boat he reached down to the water, toes curling in anticipation of the cold. But it was like getting into a bath, soft and welcoming. He stretched his arms out on either side to grip the boat, gradually eased his body down, felt the water cover his chest, his shirt sticking to his skin. Then, a big breath. He let go, pushed his arms straight out in front of him, chin on the water, and kicked furiously with his feet.

He was doing it. He was swimming.

As the dolphin came to meet him it seemed to be smiling.

THE SILLIEST OF THINGS

To look at he was a cross between George Michael and Bruce Willis: smooth and charming yet with a touch of the animal about him. He worked in Naples – had a private practice in something or other, Kelly didn't know what exactly, but it was obviously lucrative – and of course he had a house in the village. He'd pointed it out to her, balanced on a ledge high above the sea, the one with a green roof and pink shutters.

"Sometimes in autumn, when the cloud is low, you could be on a Himalayan mountain top," he'd said. *Molto romantico*. Then he'd laughed, something he did often, the kind of laugh that invites you to join in, even if you don't know what you're laughing at.

His name was Angelo. And Kelly was in love with him. True, they'd only met a week ago, but she knew. This wasn't infatuation. Or a crush. And it wasn't that she was on the rebound and over-reacting. She'd simply never felt like this before.

Of course it had a lot to do with the steamy southern Italian climate, the exotic smell of the purple wisteria draped over walls, the glitz of a sky glittering with stars. And even more with Angelo being simply the most desirable man she'd met in a long time.

All she could do was accept the madness as something inevitable, like chicken pox in childhood, and hope it didn't leave too many scars.

She toyed with all sort of ideas. Maybe she'd stay on after her holiday, send home the two bemused friends she'd arrived here with, find herself some kind of job. She'd be happy to do hotel work, serve in a bar, anything really. In the season there would be plenty of jobs. She wouldn't think about the winter.

Who knows, one day she and Angelo might marry. She'd chatted to a girl from Norway in the local *supermercato* the other day who was married to a local lad; she was tanned, and slim apart from the baby bump she rested one hand on protectively. Her smile was contagious. Kelly had heard too about an Irish girl who was getting married in a few weeks in a village high in the mountains; it sounded like just about everyone was invited, and the fireworks display – said the young waiter at the bar - would be more spectacular than an erupting Vesuvius. She loved the way they dramatised things, though she didn't much like the reminder that they were so close to an active volcano.

Would Angelo want to get married again? Once bitten and all that. He'd told her that he'd been married but it was now sadly over, he was divorced, and she believed him although she knew the local men were not to be trusted when it came to such matters. There were giveaway signs though. The way he would suddenly go quiet as though remembering someone, some other occasion, and then would shake his head, change the subject. The missing buttons on a number of his shirts. The time he'd called her by another name – Gina? Tina? – and then wouldn't stop apologising.

"Kelly, Kelly, Kelly," he'd said, no smiles this time. "Believe me, Kelly, you are the one. After just three days with you, I am reborn".

That was when she'd said yes, but well, they hardly knew anything about each other, and he'd nodded and said so we must talk.

They'd exchanged basic details. He'd grown up near Rome with four brothers, had moved to Naples when his father's work brought him south; he loved snow, hated football, could listen to opera all day but also found singers like Adriano Celentano very sexy.

"You know his voice? I have a cassette. I play for you."

She told him she'd had a solitary childhood – though with various cuddly pets so she'd never felt lonely. Her work in a bank was boring but then she liked routine. This was her first time in Italy; friends had persuaded her to join them. She hated flying; had drunk too much on the journey and felt ill for a day which was a shocking waste of a holiday, didn't he think?

He agreed.

He agreed about a lot of things: the joy of going barefooted and reading trashy magazine sometimes, and of course they both adored children. But not everything. He especially liked to cook, was sad now he only had himself to cook for. She couldn't be bothered, preferred the simplest things anyway: pasta, cheese on toast, salads. The vegetables here were a revelation. She'd tried raw fennel the other day, it was like a crisp aniseed apple she decided, delicious. *Delizioso,* he'd taught her to say. And wedges of the big bumpy local lemons that tasted sweet as oranges. A woman sitting outside her house shelling broad beans had given her a handful, told her to eat them - like this she'd said, dropping one into her own mouth and munching. They were certainly nothing like the anaemic blobs that came in tins.

Though they were together most of each day, Kelly and Angelo hadn't yet made love. They were going to this very night. Not that anything had been agreed verbally; it wasn't necessary. They both understood

"Tomorrow evening I invite you to my house," he'd said. "I will cook you a meal, something special. We will drink good wine. Afterwards, as the sky turns red, we'll sit out on the terrace and watch the fireflies."

If anyone back home had said this she'd have laughed out loud. But here, now, with this particular dark and intense man, it somehow made her knees weaken. Ridiculous, she thought. Pathetic.

"I'm looking forward to it," she said. "*Molto.*"

He'd suggested she accompany him in the morning to a town along the coast where they had the biggest fish market for miles; collected her in his grey Lancia. Curving slowly along the road cut into the side of rocks high above the sea he rested one hand lightly on the wheel, wrapped the other around hers as it lay in her lap.

If the town was like a film set with its narrow cobbled streets spanned by bridges linking houses, its amber peeling walls and pocket sized piazzas where fountains trickled, as listless as the scrawny dogs that sprawled in the dust, it had one failing. The smell of fish was everywhere. Kelly wondered if you would stop noticing it if you lived there long enough; she doubted it.

Angelo caught her arm, pointed.

"You see that shop? *E la migliore.*"

He kissed his bunched fingertips which she knew was high praise. Though she rarely ate fish - she often described herself as vegetarian, eating just a bit of fish, the occasional bacon, chicken of course - Kelly had worked briefly in a supermarket some years ago, had passed the fish counter what felt like a hundred times a day. Even so she didn't recognise any of these. They were hardly like fish, more like piles of pink and grey plastic tubing. Or silver spoons. Or multi-eyed monsters from a cartoon. Words like worms, innards, slim came to mind; the kind of words that always made her shudder.

Angelo spotted a red plastic bucket beneath a counter at the back and caught her arm. It was full of baby crabs.

"*Ecco*. Now that is something special, *non e vero*?

They were adorable; perfectly formed, pale beige, no bigger than a dandelion head, all very much alive and scrambling to get out. Every now and again one would succeed, tumbling over the edge of the bucket onto the ground. The scowling lad working in the shop would pick it up and toss it back in with the others.

"But surely…" Kelly started to say, suddenly realising what Angelo had in mind.

"They're hardly worth eating, Are they? They're so… so small."

She would have felt stupid saying she didn't want to eat them. Instead she pointed to a large and very dead fish with silvery pink scales and a sad looking eye.

"What about that one?"

"*Ma tesora*, that we can have any day. These it is rare to find."

He spoke to the boy who nodded, scooped up handfuls of the baby crabs, crammed them into a polythene bag where Kelly could see them struggling, now even more desperate. Unable to watch she went and gazed in a dress shop window.

Angelo joined her, beaming. "What a feast we're going to have tonight!"

She was about to ask what he intended to do with them – by which she meant how was he going to cook them, by which she really meant how was he going to kill them – but changed her mind. Crabs were dropped into boiling water, weren't they? Alive. She didn't want to know. And how was she going to make herself swallow them? It would be OK she supposed if he did something to them, made them look more like pieces of frozen fish steaks and less ... adorable?

Angelo tossed the bag into the back of his car, excused himself, he had to make a quick phone call. Kelly found herself unable to take her eyes off the bag which was still moving, pulsating. It reminded her of a jellyfish. For a moment she felt a mad impulse to grab the bag and race down to the beach and release the babies into rocky pools where they'd be safe.

"Couldn't we untie the bag?" she asked Angelo when he slid into the seat beside her. "So they can breathe?"

"You're so sweet," he laughed, running the back of his fingers down her cheek, bending to kiss her neck. The car's engine purred into life.

She'd been so excited about this coming night and of course she still was. But even so there was now a cloud, a niggle. The tiniest midge in the ointment.

It took forever to decide what to wear. Her two friends made unhelpful advice before heading off to a pizzeria near the beach. Eventually she settled on a simple black sundress, lots of straps so she could show off her golden skin. Big earrings of course to dress it up, bangles that clattered, shoes with heels. She tied her hair back.

She'd made another decision too.

Angelo's house was cool, dim, very modern inside with a couple of plump white sofas, a big round coffee table with a hammered copper light hung low over it, striped ethnic-looking rugs on the tiled floor, not much else. It felt like a bachelor's pad. Seductive. She could imagine him inviting other women here.

"Campari spritz, yes?"

She nodded, noticed he'd already prepared a jug of it.

He brought her drink to her, touched his glass to hers, sipped. She followed his example. She should say something now of course, but best wait until they'd finished the drink. He reached for the jug, ice cubes clunking, poured another and again she sipped and waited. She didn't feel drunk, just relaxed and a tiny bit tipsy when she suddenly found the courage to speak.

"Angelo, I know you want to cook something special for me tonight..."

"*Si*. In a minute we'll go to the kitchen, yes? I'll cook and you keep me company."

He was too enthusiastic. Why was this so important? She'd have been equally happy with spaghetti.

"Angelo, I'm so sorry, but I don't want to eat the baby crabs."

That word again. What difference did it make if they were babies or tired old fish that had been swimming around for years? Probably none of them wanted to be boiled to death.

"But of course you do. I promise you will love the taste, the texture is like..."

"No. I won't. I can't."

His smile was wavering.

"You don't like fish? But we had it I think, didn't we? A few nights ago?"

"Yes. That was different."

"How different?"

She sighed. He wasn't making this easy. Why didn't he just say fine, we'll eat something else. Or nothing. We'll forget about food and just go to bed together and make torrid love until the moon comes up, possibly until dawn.

"I can't explain. Surely we could have something else, a cheese salad or eggs, you have ...?

"*Non capisco.*" His eyes were somehow darker. "This is silly. I want tonight to be special for you. Cheese? It's what the peasants eat when they work in the fields."

Kelly couldn't believe this. They were going to have an argument, she could tell, the very air felt different. An argument about what? The silliest of things. But now it wasn't just the baby crabs. It was his attitude. Of course she didn't want a man who gave in every time she demanded something. Not every time anyway. But she did want one who could tell the difference between what was trivial and what was important to her, even if it made no sense to him. Men here were more foreign than she'd realised; he'd wanted to wine and dine her and she'd ruined it.

Worse. She'd insulted him.

He walked across to the door out onto the terrace, stood with his back to her, hands on his hips. The sun had long ago set behind the mountains, the sky now navy blue, lights coming on in houses below them. It looked like a postcard.

"Angelo, please, let me try to explain."

"No need." He turned back to her, still not smiling. "You don't want to eat my food? Fine. We'll go and have a pizza. You will be happy then?"

Kelly followed him back out to the car in silence.

The only table available was a long wooden one they had to share; the pizzas were crisp and sizzling, but both of them merely picked at the toppings. All around were packs of young people drinking cheap red wine from carafes, so boisterous it was almost impossible to speak - which was just as well as suddenly they had nothing much to say to each other. Across the room Kelly caught a glimpse of her friends who were talking to a couple of tall blonde men – Swedish probably, or German, they certainly didn't look Italian. When one of them saw her and pulled a questioning face she shook her head, mouthed that she'd tell them later.

Afterwards Kelly suggested hesitantly that Angelo drop her at the bottom of the steps that led up to her *pensione*, and he agreed. She wasn't surprised though she was disappointed. So much passion gone, dissolved in a moment.

Back in her room she kicked off her shoes, slumped down on the bed waiting for the tears to start. And waiting. But they didn't. Instead she felt suddenly flooded with relief. It was as though a spell had been broken. She was herself again, free to do what she wanted, go where her fancy took her. And to eat – she smiled at the thought – whatever she chose. Was it too late to go and find the others? Of course not. The holiday wouldn't last for ever and it would be a sin to waste a beautiful night like this staying home alone. Besides, she was starving.

DREAMLAND

She didn't see him at first, the bar being busy for mid-afternoon, surprisingly so, although bars here were not of course like pubs at home; she'd once described an Italian bar as a cross between a Wimpy, a betting shop and left luggage office. It wasn't a bad description.

But there he was again, watching her, his eyes dark and somehow too shiny. She couldn't stand it, no really. He was following her, she was sure. She finished her gin and tonic in one long gulp, the ice cubes clunking as she put down her glass, picked up her bag and headed for the door. It was a shock, the sunlight, the crowds. A tour bus passed within inches, the blast of its horn completely ignored as it edged round the curve in the road.

Her journey had exhausted her. She would go back to the hotel and sleep.

At dinner that night in the hotel's dining room, yellow gladioli in vases standing as straight as the hovering waiters, people whispering, reluctant to raise their voices over the discreet clinking of cutlery, Fran spotted him again. He was sitting a few tables away, alone like her. He had, thank goodness, changed those ridiculous striped shorts for grey trousers, a white shirt straining a bit at the buttons; his neatly cut hair had been carefully combed. She debated his age. Fifty? Or was she being unkind? His bag, the small black leather pouch on a wrist strap that she'd noticed he was carrying earlier, lay on the table beside him.

He lifted his wine glass to her. A small nod. She moved her head, neither ignoring or acknowledging his greeting. The waiter brought her *tagliatelle carbonara* which she ate nervously, aware of the man's gaze, impatient with the strands of pasta that refused to curl neatly onto her fork. Giving up she pushed aside the half full dish, brought a notebook from her bag, rummaged and found a pen. That was why she was here, after all. To make notes: the best value places to eat, what the locals drink before dinner, what sights are must-sees and how to get to them if you can't afford the arm and a leg charged by the local taxis. It was her job, what she did. Sell holidays. Right now, it was southern Italy she was writing about. At other times it was Portugal, Switzerland, Greece, wherever the package tour company she worked for chose to send her. She got paid for it too. Such an exciting, glamorous job, everyone said. Aren't you the lucky one.

How little they knew.

She'd take her coffee in the hotel bar, she decided. Later, she'd get reception to put in a call to David, tell him she'd arrived safely and that everything was fine. No, that it was wonderful, breathtakingly beautiful, that she was over the moon just to be here.

She changed her mind. To hell with him. He probably wouldn't be home anyway, he'd be out with her: his girlfriend, mistress, bit on the side. His tart.

When she started the job, he'd said that of course he didn't mind that she'd be away a lot of the time. He'd cope. He'd decorate the house, learn to cook, make his own bread even. By hand, of course. He'd get some early nights and count the days til she returned. They said don't count on it, her friends, the ones who'd dared, the ones she'd thought were far too cynical.

"Fran love, you've got to believe me. Nothing happened, nothing." That was the first lie.

"It was a stupid fling. One drunken night after work, you know how I hate coming back to an empty house, no lights on, no welcome."

The second lie. And did she detect a hint of accusation in his voice, like it was her fault?

"No. Of course I don't want you to give up the job. It's a once-in-a-lifetime opportunity, and you deserve it."

So she didn't. And despite all his promises, he didn't give her up either. Her. His younger woman

"She means nothing, Fran. Come on, she's ten years younger than me. It's...how can I explain. It's a phase. Something to do with my age. A mid..."

"Don't you dare say a mid-life crisis," That wasn't even original.

"A mistake. I made a mistake." He sighed. It sounded genuine.

"Fran, honestly, the last thing I want to do is hurt you."

She'd turned towards the window. Outside the street had glistened with the rain that had been falling for days, weeks it seemed. Drops chased each other down the glass. Summer in England. No wonder everyone was so miserable.

"If she's that important to you then go to her. If it's me you want to stay with, then break it off with her. Now. It's that simple."

He'd caught her shoulders, turned her to face him, made her look at him. She'd been surprised by the tears in his eyes.

"Listen. You have this trip planned. Go, enjoy it. I promise you that by the time you get back it will be over."

"You promise." She hesitated. "For what, the hundredth time?"

"A slight exaggeration." He gave a quick smile which she didn't return.

"OK, you're right. But this time…"

After pleading with her for an hour and three quarters – she'd timed it – David left the house. He stayed away all night. By 5am Fran had decided she'd go ahead with the trip. It was a risk: he might be gone when she got back. He might not. Sometimes you could accomplish more by doing nothing.

She'd just finished her coffee when she noticed the fat man hesitating by the door into the bar. Don't come in, please don't, she muttered under her breath, looking determinedly the other way. When she dared to look back he'd gone.

Fran slept badly, tossing to and fro in an unfamiliar bed. Peering through the half open shutters at the dazzling world outside she debated going back to bed, just for another hour. Instead she indulged in a long cool shower, found the caffeine pills that she admitted she couldn't manage without. Too many pills, too many coffees, way too much alcohol.

"Good morning. I hope you slept well?"

It was as though he'd been waiting for her outside the dining room. There was an American twang to his voice, but he wasn't American. She could smell cologne, sweet, unfamiliar; when he held the door open for her she noticed how neat and white his fingernails were.

"Would you mind if I joined you for breakfast?" How could she say yes, she would?

They were ushered to a table near the window. The sky was such a dazzling blue it hurt her eyes.

He stared out at the village below them, sighed.

"This place … it's special, no? A dreamland. You know about the pleasure park in - where is it? - Margate? Very old, very famous for its scenic railway and exotic birds and that pink fluffy..."

"Candy floss?"

"Yes. Candy floss."

Fran vaguely recollected reading something in the papers.

"Two Dutch brothers have bought it," he said. "It's good that they saved it from closing. But they changed its name which is not good."

Now she remembered. It was called Dreamland. Had been.

"You are forbidden to be unhappy in dreamland," he said.

Breakfast came at once, *cornetti* still warm to the touch, a little dish of sour cherry jam, big cups of milky coffee.

Fran started with the coffee. Her companion reached for a pastry, ate it quickly and then indicated that he'd take another, if she didn't mind?

"Go ahead. I don't eat in the morning."

His lips were voluptuous, almost feminine. Sitting next to him she felt somehow hard, her body angular, sharp. She was too thin, David said. Was she... his tart...was she soft and rounded, did her body yield beneath his, like marshmallow?

"I am from Holland." He dabbed his mouth with a napkin. "I have eight days more here."

Fran knew she had to make an effort.

"Are you here alone?"

"Yes. Sadly."

He gave a small shrug.

"Usually, for many years now, I've come with my wife and children. I have two boys and a little girl."

He added two heaped spoonfuls of sugar to his coffee

"This year there were problems. But my wife, she's an angel. She said, you've worked so hard, you need a holiday more than any of us. Go, get some sunshine, eat lots of ice cream. I can cope, she said."

He dabbed at the crumbs.

"The ice cream here is superb, don't you think? In October, they make one from the local chestnuts."

He kissed his bunched fingertips.

"You'd better watch out for the sun." Fran pushed back her chair.

"With your pale skin. You don't want to burn."

He stood too, insisted on shaking hands.

"Perhaps we will see each other this evening?"

"Perhaps. I don't know. I have lots I must do whilst I'm here."

She felt his eyes on her back as she walked away.

During the day she forgot about the man, concentrated instead on her work: first a visit to Vesuvius to edge her way around the top before peering down into what her guide insisted on describing as an over-sized ant heap. Her company always organised a guide to make getting around easier, to provide local detail. This one had been doing the job too long; he'd lost the enthusiasm she needed to find if she was to motivate her readers.

She did better at Pompei. Abandoned briefly while he chatted to a couple of taxi driver friends she referred to the book instead.

<u>On the 24th August in the year AD 79 Vesuvius erupted, burying the town of Pompei in a shower of pumice stone, a river of hot ash. Some 2,000 of its inhabitants were buried alive. Capture the horror of those last moments by visiting the gallery of plaster casts made from the original bodies so perfectly preserved: the young girl lying with her face pressed to the ground, the man who had wrapped his cloak around him for</u>

protection, the chained dog who had climbed higher and higher in a desperate bid to escape suffocation.

It was like a horror story. But she knew from past experience how people were drawn to that kind of thing, how they positively relished the gruesome details.

Back at the hotel the receptionist gave her a note along with her key. David must have called. Her tiredness fell away. She hurried to her room, wanting to be alone to unfold the thick cream sheet of paper, kicked off her shoes and sat heavily on the bed.

It was from someone called Adriaan Vestdijk.

If you would like to meet me at the fish restaurant across the road, it said, I would very much like to invite you to dinner. I shall be there from 8 onwards. I will wait for you.

She tore the note into pieces. How arrogant of him, as though she couldn't possibly decline his offer. At least she had the comfort of knowing she could drink in the hotel bar without him hovering.

After the first drink she felt calmer. Then, guilty. She couldn't just leave him sitting there, waiting. It wouldn't hurt her to go; she'd heard it was an excellent restaurant, it would be a chance to try it, maybe to include it as a recommendation when she wrote her article. And she liked fish. She thought of going up to her room to freshen up, put on some perfume, but decided against.

"I knew you'd come," he said, jumping up to pull out her chair. "You and I – we are very alike, I think."

She wanted to ask him how on earth he'd come to that conclusion, but didn't. Alike? Presumably he meant they were both lonely. Being alone didn't necessarily mean being lonely.

The restaurant was busy; their meal took forever. She made a mental note to suggest that visitors eat here early in the week when it was probably emptier. Whilst they waited Adriaan talked. About his wife, Lia, blonde like Fran and blue eyed though his wife was – he drew curves with his hands - chubbier.

"Like me, she could probably do with losing a little weight," he said, grimacing. "The trouble is, we like to eat."

About his children: Marten, Josef and Mariela. He adored them, he admitted, pulling a photograph from his bag between mouthfuls of *gambaretti*. The children were overweight too, Fran noticed. He'd left a greasy mark on one corner which she wiped away with her napkin before handing the picture back.

"You can see why I'm a happy man," he said.

"A lucky man too," Fran said, thinking she would have said the same about herself a few months ago. Even though she and David were often apart, she'd never doubted that her marriage was a good one. Strong. One that would last.

"And you," Adriaan said as though reading her thoughts. "Tell me about you."

He pushed aside his empty plate, put his elbows on the table.

She summarised. Married, no children (yet, she added, no idea why), a rambling flat in a Victorian house on the edge of the woods in north London that she hated to leave, but had to because of her work. She told him a bit about her work.

"You must be a very intelligent woman to have such a job."

Why did she find herself squirming whenever he flattered her?

"No. Just an ambitious one."

It was a good moment to plead an early start the next morning, to insist she pay half of the bill. She didn't want to be indebted to him. But he refused.

In the hotel reception he shook her hand again, holding onto it.

"I'll see you again soon, I'm sure."

She muttered excuses.

"Come on, you can find an hour or two for me," he said, head tipped to one side, a coy somehow childish gesture. "If you really want to."

In her room, creaming off make up, the tiled floor cold beneath her bare feet, the sound of laughter and vespas whizzing up the hill coming through the shutters, she thought about him. Adriaan. He irritated her, but at the same time she felt sorry for him too. No idea why. Despite his assurances that he was so happy there was a tinge of sadness about him. Neediness.

She managed to avoid him, spending her days sightseeing, making notes, the evenings translating them into selling blurb neatly typed on her much-loved Olivetti portable. She noticed that even though she hadn't had time for the beach, or even for a dip in the hotel pool, she was catching the sun; her skin glowed, her hair had new pale streaks that would have cost a fortune at the hairdressers. The early nights were doing her good too. David always said she looked great when she got back from her trips; their love-making had a new edge, at least for a week or two. She wondered what he was doing right now. Certainly not thinking of her.

Granting herself a day off she went up into the mountains behind the resort and found another village, tiny, a cluster of houses with peeling walls, flowers wilting in coffee tins outside shuttered windows. She sat on a red plastic chair outside the one small bar, drank *café freddo*. Nearby a woman who looked to be at least forty bobbed a baby on her knees, the baby gurgling with delight.

"*Che bella,*" she kept saying, kissing the scrunched-up face.

Fran asked if it was a boy or a girl.

"*Lei femina*." The mother replied.

"She is yours?"

"Si." She held up her fingers. "And I have five more."

Fran could see how proud she was.

An older woman passed them carrying a bale of hay on her back, a scarf around her head; bent double, but still she stopped to pinch the baby's cheek. Two men, deep in conversation, nodded to Fran. For the first time since arriving in Italy she heard bird song. The air sparkled with insects.

It was another world up here. Life reduced to basics. No, that sounded negative whereas Fran thought it one of the most beautiful, peaceful places she'd found on this trip. She debated writing it up for her article, then changed her mind. If she promoted it, it would be ruined. If visitors chose to make the climb, just to see what was there, and came across it by chance, lucky them.

Walking back down, she decided she couldn't wait any longer. She needed to hear David's voice. She would ring that evening.

There was no reply from the house. She thought of ringing Gill, her mother in law. They got on well, Gill was like a friend, Fran had even considered discussing it all with her, asking her what she should do. After all, she understood David better than anyone, But putting it all into words would make it too real. Better wait and see.

She too was out when Fran tried her number.

That evening there was to be an exhibition: old photos of the village recently found in a cupboard in a suitcase, damp and blotchy, photos now blown up to become works of art. As it was opening night there would be free wine, *bruschette*, a chance to meet the organiser, an advertising man from New York with links to the area. A lot of New Yorkers had links to this part of Italy. Fran had been invited. Then, as she set off, there was a cloud burst, the warm rain flooding down the steps and streets of the village so that she arrived with wet feet, even the hem of her skirt was sopping.

It didn't matter. The rain had seeped in too under the badly fitting doors of the old warehouse that was now a gallery; there were puddles where the stone paving dipped. But no-one cared, they simply circled them; local artists, tourists who had received an invitation or just dodged in to get out of the rain, important people like the mayor, and a lanky green haired pop star who had a house along the coast.

It was the kind of event Fran usually tried to avoid, pretentious, cliquey. But that was when she was home. Now she was being paid to be there. And surprisingly, the photos were good, much better than she'd expected. Simply hung against white stone walls they brought alive another era, people long gone, a time when it was a fishing village not a sophisticated resort. David would have loved them. He liked old black and white photos best, said they were honest.

David, David, David.

She was furious with herself, for the way she had to bring him into everything.

"Ah ha. Found you."

Even before she turned she knew who it was. He stood there, fingers wrapped around an empty wine glass that he held close to his chest, leaning towards her with a smile on his shiny face.

"Adriaan. Well. So what do you think?"

"Of you? I love that dress. The blue is absolutely..."

"Of the photos."

He stood back, cast a dismissive eye over the walls.

"Interesting, I guess. Not real art, of course"

He reached to take a *bruschetta* from a plate being handed around by a young girl in shorts and stiletto heels, then took another.

"Here. Eat this. I'm starving, aren't you? Shall we go and find some proper food? There's a restaurant..."

"No, I couldn't eat any more tonight."

"You've eaten so early?"

She hadn't but had no intention of confessing.

"A drink then. Away from this rabble."

"No, I..."

"One. A pretty pink cocktail perhaps?"

Cornered, she nodded. A quick one. She made the usual excuses.

"You are always in a hurry, or tired, or both," he said as he caught her elbow and edged her through the crowd towards the door. She felt admonished.

At least the rain-washed streets felt cool. Over *negronis* he said he would be going home at the end of the week, was looking forward to seeing his family again. Beautiful as it was here, he missed them.

"I admit, I'm lonely. At night especially. I lie there in my big empty bed and look at the ceiling and wait for morning, and sometimes I think it will never come. When did nights get to be so long? Sometimes – often I take sleeping pills."

"I know what you mean." Fran said it before she could stop herself.

Adriaan reached and spread his hot hand over hers.

"You do? You see, I was right. We understand each other, you and I".

She left her hand on the table briefly, then pulled it away and pretended to be searching for something in her bag.

"Another drink?"

"No. Really"

"Of course you will." He waved to the waiter, indicated two more.

She drank hers quickly, concerned about the slur in his voice, though the bar was filling up and it was hard to hear anything much over the chatter and bursts of laughter. She wished she was with them – the others who seemed to be having such fun together. Every now and again Adriaan would tail off into silence and just sit there, staring at her.

She insisted they go. He emptied his glass, stood unsteadily.

On the walk back to the hotel he caught her hand and linked it through his arm. She didn't want to hold onto him but sensed it was more that he needed her support. Wasn't it? He pulled her closer and she could smell alcohol. His bag, still suspended from his wrist, hit against her as they maneuvered the slippery steps.

There was no message for her.

They walked together to the waiting lift. The doors slid silently closed.

Adriaan draped his arm across her shoulders.

"Don't look so sad. You're too beautiful to be so sad."

She tried to shrug free.

"I know. An idea. You come to my room with me, I will make you happy."

He lowered his arm, took her hand in his and pressed her palm against the bulge in his trousers.

Fran wasn't sure whether to scream or laugh.

As the lift doors opened he tugged her through them before she'd realized what was happening. He was stronger than she'd expected.

"Come."

For heaven's sake, what was he thinking?

"Adriaan. This is ridiculous."

He'd stopped by a door, was trying with difficulty to get the key into the lock, still holding onto her wrist. His breathing was heavy.

"This is silly. Let go, now, before..."

The door was swinging open. He turned to her, hesitated, then let her go, instead cupping her face with his hands.

"Please, my dear. Please come with me, Just for a while. We can help each other, I know we can. We're both alone on this beautiful night, why not?"

"Because I don't want to," Fran snapped, shaking free of his hands. "Because you're married and I'm married, and even if I wasn't, why would I want to have sex with a slimy toad like you..."

His face crumpled. Fran turned away and ran back to the waiting lift, pressed the button for her floor, her heart pounding.

Back in her room she stood with her back to the door in the darkness, the polished wood cool against her bare arms. Even as she fumed at his arrogance she wondered how she could have been so cruel. A toad? And anyway, they're not slimy, are they?

Next morning she had coffee brought up to her, hurried out the moment reception rang to say her guide had arrived. It was going to be a long, hot day: she had ten or more hotels to visit, details to be collected, checked and double checked. It was the part of the job she disliked most, the boring part, but it had to be done.

It was evening before she got back to the hotel. As she walked into reception she could sense at once that something had happened. People we gathered in clusters, talking about it in that hushed, excited way people talk about such events. There had been a death in the hotel: the Dutchman. Such a shame. Such a nice polite man. He'd been drinking, had taken sleeping pills. The police were unsure if it was an accident or intentional. Or maybe he'd had a heart attack.

Despite the heat Fran began to shiver. He'd taken pills, she was sure of it. Maybe not intending to kill himself, but with all that alcohol swishing around his body. But it wasn't her fault, how could it be? She hardly knew the man. She wasn't responsible for him, for his happiness. Was she?

And then there was the wife. Suddenly it seemed important to Fran that she contact his wife, say that she'd known him, that they'd enjoyed a few drinks together, talked. She would tell her that he'd seemed to be enjoying his time here in... what had he called it? His little paradise?

She asked the young man in reception if the police had been in touch with his wife yet.

"His wife? No, *signora*. You make a mistake. He has no wife."

"But of course he has. He comes here every year with her and his..."

"*Si, signora.* He comes here every year, but always alone. He jokes that he is still looking for the right woman."

He glanced down, gave a small shrug.

"A very lonely man, I think."

Fran turned away.

"*Un momento, signora.*" He held out a folded piece of paper.

"Here. Your husband telephoned earlier. He left this message."

It said: <u>Everything sorted. Come home now, please, right away, I beg you</u>.

Fran blinked. It wasn't going to be that simple. New starts and all that sounded easy but could she do it? Could David? At least they could give it a try.

"*Signora*? It is not bad news, I hope?"

"No," she said. "No, everything's fine."

She managed a smile as she turned towards the bar, unable to wipe the picture of Adriaan's sad, hurt, lost face from her mind.

THE SWIFTS OF AMALFI

The swifts were a surprise, a dozen, maybe more, zipping back and forth like black arrows against an azure sky, so high they were almost invisible, making Rachael look up so that she stumbled as she got out of the taxi.

Careful, she muttered. How embarrassing if she fell flat on her face.

Of course she'd have come by bus if she'd been doing it on her own. By which she meant paying for herself. Lee had arranged for a taxi to meet her at the airport and so she'd had no need to rough it. The driver was standing there on the other side of the barrier, a piece of cardboard held in front of him: TAXI FOR MISSIS GIBSON scrawled in thick black pen. His sharp eyes watched the faces of passengers as they filed past him weighed down with suitcases and no-longer needed jackets, waiting for someone to acknowledge him. When she did his smile was quick and wide enough to show teeth missing on both sides. He dabbed at his brow with a scarf, stuffed it into his pocket and tugged the bulging bag out of her hand; she'd planned on travelling light, it was just a long weekend, had no idea what was in it.

"This way, please, missis," he said, setting off to weave a brisk path through the crowds. She struggled to keep up, not yet over the flight, her ankles beginning to puff up, the thick hot air making it hard to breathe. Outside the light was dazzling; she shouldn't have packed her sunglasses in her overnight bag. Stupid thing to do.

Sitting in the back of the taxi with all the windows down she began to feel better. The driver had tried to make conversation but neither of them understood each other so with an apologetic shrug he'd given up. The *autostrada* was busy: it was as if they were in a river being swept along by a current of cars, all moving too fast. Rachael closed her eyes. She slept.

It was as they were rounding a hairpin bend on the steep hill from Amalfi up to Ravello that she came suddenly awake. On either side were never-ending lemon groves, gnarled wooden trellises covered with mat-like wads of green leaves protecting the pendulous yellow fruits that hung motionless below. Rachael had read about the famous Amalfi lemons, couldn't wait to try them. She wanted to try other things too: pastries, *gelati* of course, drinks with names like *finochietto* and *averna.*

It was going to be fun, her first holiday without the children. No-one to take messages for, to drive to the station or pick up from parties, to worry about, secretly and continually. She could be as selfish as she wanted. This was to be her time.

No doubt about it, she'd done the right thing in coming.

Hadn't she?

The hotel was small but perfect. It oozed quality, style, money. Inside the entrance hall the first thing she noticed was the hand painted ceramic tiled floor, sweeps of herbs strewn underfoot; it felt almost sacrilege to step on it in scruffy sandals.

The woman behind the desk asked politely for her passport, tucked it in a drawer, turned a key.

"Is safe. I return to you this evening, yes?"

Rachael nodded. The woman emerged from behind the counter, beckoned.

"We have reserved two of our best rooms for you," she said, leading the way up a flight of stone stairs, Rachael following, a young man following behind with her bag.

"This one for you," she said, pushing wide the unlocked door. The room was cool, dim; a thin white curtain billowed in the disturbed air.

"This," she added, one red tipped finger pointing at a door opposite "is for your friend, Signor Trent."

So he'd reserved two rooms. Rachael was relieved and yet - in a way - disappointed too. It suddenly struck her that he'd been here before with someone else, possibly more than once. Why not? He was a single man, charming, worldly. He met new people all the time.

Pontone is perfect, he'd written in loosely looped letters, dark blue ink. It's small but pretty; winding lanes, a fountain, church, all the usual. A few good places to eat if we don't want to go to Ravello or Amalfi. Best of all, even in late summer it's not too crowded.

Alone in the room Rachael kicked off her sandals, went out onto the balcony which was crammed with flowers in pots, a sudden riot of hot colours: reds, purples, flame-like oranges. No sign of the swifts. She was disappointed.

*

A deep breath, and then count; one, two, three, four, five. Lee hated to show any sign of impatience, used to say it was never necessary, bad manners, the sign of a weak boss. But for god's sake. He'd planned everything, no detail overlooked, determined that he'd leave the office by early afternoon. His flight from Fiumicino was at four and he had no intention of missing it. He'd wanted everything to be perfect.

And now, this.

The dusty office window was open, a motorbike's roar breaking through the continual rumble of the city's traffic. He'd had enough of it; he longed to be somewhere quiet, deserted, where the air smelt of green things not petrol and urine. Right now he hated Rome. He crossed to the window, slammed it shut knowing they'd all be hotter than they already were within minutes. He'd worked in New York for a while, had got used to air conditioning; Rome may be full of beautiful old buildings but they were hell to work in.

His assistant was still standing patiently by his desk, eyes lowered, waiting for instructions. Lee reminded himself that she was only passing on the news, not responsible for the missing consignment.

"OK," he said, dropping into the swivel chair behind the desk, running his finger along inside his shirt collar. He reached for his cigarettes, shook one out of the pack.

"We'd better start making some phone calls."

*

Rachael knew she had a decision to make, a big one, one that could – would - affect so many lives. But not yet. Instead she would get some fresh air, stretch her legs. Be a real tourist and go sightseeing.

You can walk down to Amalfi, the receptionist told her. Seven hundred and fifty steps, top to bottom, she added. Maybe Rachael should have heeded the warning.

It seemed never-ending, step after step after step, sometimes going through groves or chestnut woods, others so close to people's houses that she felt embarrassed to be intruding on their privacy, though the few she saw – mostly black-clad and elderly - simply nodded and then ignored her. From an open window she heard a child singing the scales, someone accompanying him slowly, patiently on a piano. How on earth did they get that up here? she wondered.

She'd forgotten what it felt like to be so hot, to perspire so much that her blouse was clinging to her skin. At least she'd located her sunglasses, was pleased too that she'd brought with her an old floppy hat found in a charity shop, way too outlandish to wear under the grey skies of home. There was a blister forming on at least one toe.

Not far now.

The music reached her ears just as she reached town. Bagpipes? Surely not? She headed on down the cobbled street, shops on either side opening after the siesta, wooden shutters clattering as they were raised. Nearer the main square she could hear laughter, chattering, obviously a large crowd of people who knew each other well.

It was a wedding party, A cluster of young men in black suits, white shirts and polished shoes flirted with girls in clinging green dresses that brushed the dusty pavement. The bride and groom stood hand in hand in front of a tall fountain in the centre of the piazza, two couples Rachael decided were their parents hovering nearby waiting to be placed by the photographer. Holiday makers in shorts dawdled past; when the couple were instructed to kiss, there was a ripple of applause. Both the groom and the bagpipe player wore kilts; obviously not local then. Getting married in far-flung places was all the rage, it seemed. For those who could afford it of course.

Rachael turned away, found a shady side street and a table outside a bar. Weary now, she sat with her back to the wall, asked the young man who came to take her order what he'd suggest. Without hesitation he said a *granita di limone*. She nodded, hoped he'd bring it quickly, whatever it was.

Weddings. So many expectations. Of the day, the honeymoon, the life you'll share as a couple, your kids, your dreams. You think it will all go right, you have every confidence. You never think that one still and misty autumn morning the man you love will get out of bed and vomit. And vomit again and again until he's sent for tests that reveal he has cancer, and three months to live. And that come Christmas you and the twins will be having to put up the Christmas tree without his help. Rachael had never before realized how difficult it was to get a bulky tree into a car, and then indoors, and then get it to remain upright whilst you tie on a hundred fiddly, twinkly ornaments.

Not that they'd had a big wedding, she and Tony. It wouldn't have felt right, not under the circumstances. They were both more than happy to make their vows in a registry office, to go for fish and chips afterwards.

The waiter was back.

"That looks amazing."

In fact it looked like a dish of crushed ice and for a moment she felt an urge to plunge her fingers into it, or better still, her feet.

"Very refreshing," the young man said, hovering by her side, anxious for her to try it. She picked up the long spoon. The lemon ice melted instantly on her tongue.

Overhead a sudden piercing scream, swifts criss-crossing the wedge of sky between the tall buildings, skimming roof tiles. There seemed to be so many of them whizzing around that Rachael began to feel dizzy.

"*I rondoni*," the waiter said, following her gaze. "I like very much. You too? Once one fell..."

He indicated something found at his feet.

"I pick up, he is warm, so light, a handful of feathers."

"Poor thing," she said.

"So still, but breathing. I keep in box overnight. This man – how you say, *uno esperto*? – he tell me it may just have knocked against something, yes? He say go on my t*errazza*, hold up my hands, like this, and then wait."

"And?"

Rachael could see he'd told the story many times. He smiled, shrugged.

"He fly. So quickly I hardly see him go."

She imagined the moment, the exhilaration.

"I love them too. I hate it when they leave to fly south."

"These, they're going soon I think. They are very ... agitated? Is the word?"

"Bet you miss them. I would. I do, the few we have back home. It's horrid when they leave."

A couple with two red-faced children and a grizzling baby in a pushchair slumped down at a nearby table. The waiter turned to attend to them.

"Yes, but they come back," he said over his shoulder. "Always they come back."

The *granita* was fast becoming a bowl of slush.

*

Lee asked for ice with his whisky. He usually drank it neat but probably a good idea to have it watered down; it was his third. The airport bar was crowded but somehow he'd managed to get himself a stool at the end of the counter, felt he'd been perched there forever.

Did Rachael drink whisky? He couldn't remember. To be honest he couldn't remember so many of the details: what she liked to eat, what music she enjoyed, if she was a morning person or came alive at night. They'd had a few short weeks together. Strange about time, though; he could still recall the way she'd made him feel, this gentle girl in the flower-embroidered smock, her hesitant smile, the feel of her long brown hair as it touched his skin; she'd liked to wrap it around his neck like a scarf. It was a good time to be young, the best, a time of flower power, free love; the Beatles singing about a day tripper and no-one knowing if they meant LSD or a prostitute, or caring. A very special time.

He couldn't believe his bad luck, meeting her just before he was due to go to America to work in a kids' summer camp. He asked her to go with him, begged her, but she wouldn't. She said she wasn't a traveller, she liked the familiar, had no need for novelty.

"You go," she'd said, "Have your adventures."

"I'll be back in the autumn."

"And then, didn't you say you were going to work in a ski resort?"

"I am." A pause. "I was."

"Lee, do what's right for you. It's been great but I don't want to change you, that would be wrong. Besides, it wouldn't work. Eventually you'd blame me for – I don't know – ruining your life or something."

She was right. As she so often was.

So he'd gone, and at first had spent his evenings squeezing as much news as he could onto a single crinkly blue airletter.

But then – as he settled into his new life - his days became busier, his free time more precious. Her replies seemed to take longer too. So it wasn't entirely his fault that they'd lost touch, was it? He'd regretted it though. Often. More often than he'd have admitted.

Twist of fate then that they'd bumped into each other in the snow just after last Christmas, strings of lights across the street already lit up though it was mid-afternoon. He was back in the small county town where he'd grown up – where they both had, of course – but he'd been back before and never seen her. And she too had moved away, it seemed, had come back for a family get-together.

Forget coincidence: this was meant to be.

They'd hardly recognized each other, both wrapped top to toe in thick coats, boots, scarves flapping in the wind. Then again, he'd never have forgotten those grey-blue eyes, the slightly quizzical curve of one eyebrow. She'd recognized him by his – what he called regal - nose which they'd agreed was the best thing about his face.

"Lee? Is that really you in there?"

"It is. But I'm not removing anything to prove it."

They'd stood chatting only briefly, both stamping their feet as the cold seeped up their legs.

"I have to go."

"Me too."

Neither of them had moved.

"But… well, can we stay in touch? Look, I'll give you my address." Lee tugged off a glove, unbuttoned his coat and dug into a pocket.

"Here's my card. I'm living in Rome right now."

"Lucky you," she'd said, taking it from him.

"You will write, won't you?" he'd said. "Promise?"

She'd nodded, but he hadn't been sure until the first letter arrived; he'd carried it around with him like a teenager with a crush.

He was joggled aside by someone determined to get to the bar, downed the melted ice water. And finally, at long last, the announcement he'd been waiting for: his flight to Naples was boarding. He slid off the seat, picked up his luggage bag.

*

Back in her darkening hotel room Rachael stood in front of the mirror. She thought she looked middle aged, tired, her hair lank and in need of washing even though she'd showered that morning before leaving home.

She put her fingers on either side of her face and pulled the skin back gently; five years younger, just like that. She let it go again. She closed her eyes.

What was Lee expecting of her anyway?

His letters since they'd met had been so easy, so chatty that she could hear his voice as she read them. She'd hoped he'd suggest meeting up again, and also dreaded it. And then when he came up with the idea of a long weekend on the Amalfi coast she'd had no choice but to say yes.

But twenty years: that's a lifetime. They were different people then. She'd read once that nearly all the atoms in a human body are renewed every year, that in five years every single part – the skin, the liver, the skeleton, the toenails, all of it – is brand new. Except for teeth, she seemed to remember, though she'd no idea why that was. She'd thought then that it was a wonder anyone ever recognized anyone after so long, let alone knew the workings of their mind.

A knock at the door. Flustered suddenly, she ran her fingers through her hair, glanced at her watch. Lee wasn't due for another hour.

It was the receptionist.

"I have a message from Mr Trent. He is sorry but he has been delayed. He will be here as quickly as he can."

It came back to Rachael suddenly, his terrible sense of timing, always trying to squeeze more into each day than was possible. She smiled.

"Thank you."

So much for the special evening meal he'd promised. And her tummy was already rumbling. She asked if it would be possible to have a sandwich brought up to her, immediately regretted the pleading tone she'd used.

"*Si. Subito.*"

But really, she could get used to this way of living. Half an hour out on the terrace with her snack, then she'd lie down for a while before taking a long refreshing shower.

*

He found her in the hotel gardens beneath an almost full moon, music from somewhere down below in the village, jazz, or bossa nova which she hasn't heard for years. She was sitting on a swing seat and moving gently to and fro. When he appeared in the doorway – the light behind him so he was no more than a dark figure, jacket slung over one shoulder - she at first wasn't sure it was Lee. He spotted her instantly.

"Rachael, love, what can I say? I'm so sorry."

He came to her, caught her hands and held her away from him as he looked her up and down.

"You look stunning," he said. "Love the short hair, it suits you."

"And you look shattered."

He shrugged.

"Business. It's been a hell of a day. But I'm here now. Let's go and eat, shall we?"

"Surely they're not still serving food?"

"Let's see."

The restaurant was empty, in semi darkness except for a round table in the middle with a pale green tablecloth, set with cutlery, napkins, white candles burning in a tall pewter candelabra.

A waiter in a white jacket pulled back the chair for Rachael, then took a bottle from an ice bucket, wrapped a napkin around its neck as he opened it.

"You organized all this?"

"You like it?"

"Are you serious?"

They ordered. They ate. They sipped *prosecco*, one that tasted nothing like the supermarkets ones she splashed out on for special occasions. They talked, though Rachael suddenly realized the talk was mostly about her: her life, her marriage, the twins.

On the far wall she could see them reflected in a floor to ceiling mottled mirror, imagined they were strangers: two attractive people in their middle years, comfortable with each other. They looked right together.

She took charge of the conversation.

"So. This high-powered business you run."

"It's nothing. It makes me a living. You don't want to know about it."

"Try me."

He sighed.

"It sounds unbelievable," she went on. "I mean, why would ex pats living here need to import food when they're surrounded by all this?"

"It's about nostalgia, the foods they grew up with, that remind them of occasions or people."

"Like?"

"You want a list? OK. Tea-bags, Marmite, Cadbury's Chocolate."

"The chocolate I can understand."

"Bachelor's Snackpots – ever eaten them? Looks like woodchip. You add water."

Rachael pulled a face.

"Aero. Angel Delight. Fig rolls."

"Actually, that's enough. I'm beginning to feel queasy."

"Know what they've got a passion for in Florence? Parma Violets. Remember them? Little chips of rock that taste like soap."

The candles flickered as the waiter came to the table, shared the last trickle of wine between the two glasses. As he left the room they could hear voices through the briefly open door, then it shut and the only sound was the crickets chirping outside.

A pause.

"I love that sound, don't you?" she said. "Reminds me of those water sprinklers they use on bowling greens."

"Love the taste. Had some in Africa, deep fried. Scrumptious."

What were they going on about? They were like teenagers on a first date.

Rachael put her hand on top of his. He was as nervous as she was.

"Anyway..." His tone changed.

His fingers curled around hers. He didn't look at her, kept his eyes on their hands.

"Anyway, I'm thinking of going back to England, getting a grown-up job. Doing something that matters for once."

Rachael didn't know what to say. Or rather, she didn't dare say what she felt in case she'd got it wrong, was reading things into his words that weren't there.

"Why would you give up all this?"

"What? Being a bachelor? Roaming the world? Sounds good, huh? But believe me, it's not all it's hyped up to be. Not once you pass forty anyway."

She pulled her hand free.

She did – finally – know what she was going to do. For days she'd been thinking about it. Her chair scraped noisily on the tiled floor as she stood.

"Sorry, there's something... I won't be a moment."

The receptionist and a man in an apron who looked like a chef were behind the desk watching TV, some kind of quiz show, looked up as she indicated she wanted to make a phone call. The cabin in the corner of reception was dark and airless, but still she pulled the door tight.

When she returned to the table Lee looked quizzical but didn't ask.

"So, what were you saying?" Rachael nudged, needing to hear him say it again.

At their bedroom doors she turned to him. He tucked a strand of her hair behind her ear, bent and kissed her lightly on the cheek. Not for the first time she noticed the cologne he was wearing. Italian men liked to smell good; she hoped he wouldn't lose that habit.

"Sleep well, love."

His door shut before she'd even opened hers.

*

For Mark, this was paradise. Leaving the site whilst the sky was still a dusky pink, settling into his old Fiat – third hand, probably fourth – with its top down so that the warm wind could ruffle his hair. Right at this moment he couldn't think of anything he'd rather be doing, even if he did have a long drive ahead of him. It would be a beautiful drive, up from the south where he'd been working for the summer, along the edge of the sea towards the Amalfi coast where work for most people – the indulgent, pleasure-seeking foreigners at least - was a dirty word. *La dolce vita*, wasn't that what they called it? Not for him of course. Boring. Right now he loved working on the archaeological site, digging, sifting, getting dusty and weary. Spending the evenings drinking *birra peroni* with other volunteers, enthusiasts from far flung places: grizzled old archaeologists, teachers and nurses taking a break to recover their sanity. A couple of flirty younger girls who insisted on wearing shorts even though there was a danger of snakes; a viper had been found curled under a cupboard in the site kitchen only a few weeks ago.

He'd been asked if he'd stay on for the winter. He wasn't sure. He had things to see, to do, to experience. Itchy feet, as Rachael would say. Did say, often.

He'd no idea why she'd rung so late at night to ask him to come and meet her, except of course that she was staying reasonably nearby and they hadn't seen each other for months.

"Come for breakfast," she'd said.

It was more of a command than an invitation, not at all like her.

He slowed to avoid a flock of sheep skittering around, a man on a pedal bike and his dog doing their best to usher them to the side. When finally Mark managed to squeeze past the man raised his stick in greeting.

*

The swifts had gone.

Rachael stood on the balcony and listened to the silence. There had been times over the last day when she couldn't exactly hear them, but she'd known they were still around. Now there was something different. A vacuum. It was as though a hole had opened in the sky and they'd been sucked up into it and the hole had been closed.

"Bye," she muttered. "See you again next year."

A small cough behind her. Lee was standing there looking apologetic. She'd forgotten how attractive he was. Not handsome, his face was too craggy for handsome.

"I'm sorry. I knocked on your door, then when you didn't answer I tried the handle and..."

"Don't worry," she said. "I'm not about to scream for help."

After what he'd said last night – about moving back to the UK, about hoping they would see more of each other, that he'd really like that, about his missing her, wanting to get in touch over all the years - she'd lain awake for hours. But instead of exhausted she felt calm, as though everything had slotted into place.

"Shall we go down for breakfast, or have it sent up?"

She shook her head.

"Let's go down."

In the end neither of them felt like eating. They took their *cappuccinos* outside, stretched out on the loungers beside the pool. They had the place to themselves, other visitors already off on day trips or heading for the beach.

"Where shall we go today then? I've got lots…"

"Let's stay here, just for a while," Rachael said, the sparkling pool water making her squint. She put on her sunglasses. "The thing is… I hope you don't mind but I've asked someone to join us."

She could feel him looking at her, waiting for her to go on. She didn't.

"Whatever you want," he said then.

He dug in his pocket for his cigarettes, then put the pack down without opening it. Probably about time he gave up smoking.

The smell of jasmine from the hedge behind them was almost overpowering.

Rachael closed her eyes, took some deep breaths.

"Mum?"

For a moment she thought she was asleep and dreaming, then from the hotel steps on the other side of the pool someone waved at her, a tall skinny young man in jeans and T-shirt with a mop of dusty hair.

"Shall I swim across or run round?" he called.

He didn't wait for an answer but plunged straight into the water, arms curving up and then down as he swam easily across to where she now stood, waiting. He hauled himself out, shook like a dog, and Rachael laughed as she backed away from the cold droplets. But then she reached for him and hugged him close.

"You're crazy, Mark!"

She turned to where Lee was now standing too, staring, smiling, though she could see that the smile had become more of a question mark. Then he slowly shook his head. He knew, she could see it. Or he half knew. He suspected.

She was going to have to say something.

"Mark, this is…"

"It's him, isn't it?"

She loved her son for the way he hesitated just a moment, and then the grin started.

"I'm right. I know I am."

He'd known of course that Tony wasn't his real father, his birth father - she'd told him years ago. But that was all she'd said. No explanation, no name. And though he'd thought about it often enough he hadn't asked. Give it time, he'd decided. She'd tell him when she was ready.

So this was the moment.

"Bloody hell," was all he could manage. He ran both hands through his hair.

Rachael turned to Lee.

"Lee, I couldn't tell you, couldn't tie you down," she said. "Maybe I was wrong but… and then when I met Tony and he accepted Mark as his own …"

"Stop Rachael. Please. Don't say another word."

He seemed unable to move. The three of them stood there. A wisp of cloud passed over the sun and for a moment there was a shiver in the air, then it moved on.

Lee found his voice.

"I never dreamt of this," he said. "Not once. I'm shocked, and moved and... and, how can I describe it? Happy doesn't begin to do it."

He reached out with both arms, put one around Rachael, the other around Mark's wet shoulders, pulled them both close. Rachael thought how she'd been there just one day – less than a day – and already her life had changed so much, and for the better. Better than she'd dared to hope.

The Amalfi coast magic, perhaps?

POSTCARDS

"I'm not leaving you, Gail," he said, stopping briefly to turn and give her a quick placatory smile. He was packing, flinging things into a suitcase in his usual way, the way he approached life, spontaneously, without plan or fuss.

"Two months. Three at the most and I'll be back."

"So this is what... an extended holiday?"

"Come on, please let's not go over it again," he said as he checked his pocket for air tickets, traveller's cheques, his passport: Philip Lewis, Citizen of the United Kingdom and Colonies, occupation artist.

"It's something I need to do. I have to do."

He looked tired. Too many nights spent arguing. Her fault of course, she was too conventional, too uptight. She should understand that he was an artist and artists need space. Freedom. Challenges.

He closed the suitcase, locked it with a noise like an exclamation mark.

"Sweetheart, you know I'm crazy about you. You do, don't you? If we really love each other, being apart will only make our love stronger."

Sure, he loved her. And for some obscure and completely illogical reason, she loved him too.

But this wasn't about love. What he meant was that she must learn not to cling, not to have dinner waiting on the table. Not to want marriage nor even commitment. Not to tie him down. It was a lesson.

She swallowed the hurt, felt it lodge somewhere deep inside. She would cope with it later. In his company she was her usual self, bright and silly as the red dungarees she wore to clash with her tousled orange hair. To prove she could manage, would be fine without him, she'd enrolled for juggling classes, bought tickets for a series of talks on learning to appreciate Baroque music, rang her sister in Yorkshire and arranged a visit.

When he left she kissed him lightly, turned away in case her eyes gave her away.

"I'll send you a postcard," he said. "Every day. Promise."

Typical. He couldn't even commit to writing her letters.

"I hope you find it," she said.

"It?"

"Whatever it is that's missing from your life."

"Me too," he said. Sighed, as he walked away.

He was renting a room in the village by the sea, taking pen and paper, intending to do sketches, watch sunsets, maybe meditate a little. To re-discover himself. Get back to his roots. His mother had been Italian, had taught her son little of the language but had passed on an instinctive feel for the way of life, a love of the people, an understanding of their moods, their melancholy. He blamed his mercurial temperament on his Italian blood.

And he felt at home at once. He'd been to the village a couple of times before; people remembered his long thin face, his hair tied back with a rubber band, a sketchpad always under his arm. Some remembered his name. *"Ciao Filippo,"* they nodded as they passed on the steps that ambled between houses with walls peeling like onion skin, doors gaping to reveal gloomy rooms where women in black sat shelling peas. They were forever cooking, or shopping for food. Or feeding fat babies who suckled greedily at their full, olive-skinned breasts.

"*Ciao,*" he replied, and then would stop and talk a while about this and that, nothing special, gossip. It made him feel he belonged, was part of village life. It was a good feeling.

He started sketching at once.

During the day the sun shone relentlessly, no longer yellow but the same dark gold that was everywhere, tipping the few sparse trees, ferns, the shrubs that clung to the mountain slopes behind the village. It was autumn. Still it was hot. He sought the shade, shared it with old men and dogs.

Early evenings he would reward himself with a swim in a sea that was warm, still, as clear as the white wine he would drink later outside a bar, at a table on the pavement, usually alone and content to be so. Passing conversations were one thing, but he shied away from close contact, didn't want to hear about the things that kept people awake at night: unmarried daughters, unexplained lumps, mushroom-like worries that grew in the dark. He must be free to solve his own problems. Whatever they may be; sometimes he wondered if he didn't have a tendency to create them rather than solve them. Wondered if he actually needed problems in order to feel alive.

Four days after arriving Philip wrote Gail a postcard. He'd arrived safely, was settled already, had found a huge oak door that demanded to be sketched, a wrought iron lantern hanging over it draped with the strangest greenery, like seaweed. The house itself was so old it was crumbling. Undoubtedly haunted by the ghosts of wealthy Neapolitans. JUST UP YOUR STREET, he added.

He thought of the terraced house he shared with her, two up two down, nothing special but it was on the edge of town, they could see fields from the upstairs window, grass dappled with black and white cows. Missing the cool he thought of autumn days in England, soft and grey as a pigeon's neck. He missed birds too; there were none here except a few scraggy blackbirds in cages.

But there are compensations, he reminded himself. Food was one. He re-discovered the pleasure of eating, tried different restaurants, one no more than a hole in the wall where there was no menu, the cook serving whatever he felt like cooking that day, standing over you, watching as you ate.

"You like?" It would have been hard to say no, see the smile slip from his shiny face. It would also have been unlikely. He was an excellent cook. The only time Philip complained was when one of the many stray cats that loitered optimistically in the doorway was sick under his table.

"*Non importa,*" shrugged the waiter, a plump scowling boy. Philip moved to another table.

On the beach the restaurants were more expensive, with thick ivory napkins matching the tablecloth. Here he ate French crêpes, Mexican chilli. Cats were shooed away.

He found a postcard showing a long wooden table set amidst trees, a family at dinner, peasants with the rounded arms and rosy cheeks of people who enjoy eating and drinking. He couldn't resist it, wrote on the back I'M GETTING FAT which, if not quite true, would be before long. When he got back he'd have to watch his weight. Back to England, back to his real work: engraving weeds, grasses, fungi onto metal plates to be made into prints, framed, sold in craft shops. When he was lucky. Though a review of a show he'd had in a local café praised his sharp eye and delicate touch, it was hard to find people who appreciated his art enough to actually buy something. He'd thought of giving up, changing to a different medium, though

Gail dissuaded him. She had faith in his talent, believed that things happened in their own time. Be patient, she said.

Gail. He looked at his watch, calculated the hour in England. Wondered what she would be doing at that precise moment.

There was a *festa* on the beach one night, everything free, fish, wine, bread. Local children sang and danced shyly to Neapolitan folk songs, tripping over skirts borrowed from older sisters, banging tambourines. Someone strummed a sitar, a young Italian who had studied in India.

Then, a mood change. From a cassette player came the American pop songs played continuously on the radio back home, and now young girls danced with each other, dogs barking, boys throwing bits of bread to attract attention. More wine was produced. Philip leant against a rock enjoying it all without being part of it; the nervous flickering fires, the laughter, louder as the night went on, the whole scene lit by a full moon. People enjoying each other's company as they had through the centuries. Nothing more was needed.

He thought of a street theatre group he'd recently become involved with, performing mime on village greens to tiers of people, young children in front, their parents behind them, boys balanced precariously on the branches of trees. He enjoyed it as much as the audience did. Gail performed too, she was good at it, had a way with children. Had a talent for speaking with her hands, eyes, the way she moved. It was when she put things into words that the misunderstandings began. Or when he did.

There were suddenly people in the room next door to Philip, a young French couple with a baby. He resented it, used to his privacy, the only sounds being the distant coughing of the landlord downstairs, his wife singing to herself as the stirred the lentil puree they seemed to eat every day. Catching glimpses of the newcomers on the stairs, in front of the house as they struggled to unfold the chair they wheeled the baby about in, Philip nodded briefly. Hippy was the word that came to mind, an old-fashioned word, but then there was something dated about them: the black clothes they wore, their scruffiness, beads around their neck, entwined with the girl's long hair. The smell of the hash they smoked wafted under the interconnecting doors. He found himself worrying about the baby, about whether such casual parents made good ones. They seemed to like giving the baby baths, or maybe it was just a way to keep him quiet, to change his cries to giggles, splashes. Philip could hear him through the thin walls.

One morning he bumped right into the girl, couldn't avoid speaking to her. Her English was faultless. She said the baby would be a year old next day, and that they were going to buy a cake, a small one, just big enough for a single candle. They hadn't money for cakes, she said, had spent it all on getting away from Paris for a week. They'd had to, her husband was unwell, his heart, he'd been working too hard, taking everything too seriously. She smoothed the baby's hair as she talked. Philip felt a twinge of guilt. It wasn't for him to make judgements, it was none of his business.

He thought about babies, children, families, the awful responsibility of it all. The young French couple seemed happy enough. But he wasn't ready. Not yet. Maybe never.

He sent Gail another postcard, mentioned the neighbours, their baby. Something made him add his address. He'd left it, but maybe she'd lost it. Not that he expected her to write, but just in case she wanted to.

As the days shortened, the nights got colder. He needed a blanket on the bed. The village started to empty, the last few tourists heading back to towns where there were smoke-filled bars, cinemas, strip joints and jostling crowds to keep winter at bay. Some of the hotels and *pensiones* were already closed. On the beach the bars were being boarded up, chairs folded and stored in the now empty cabins. Though there was a sadness about the place, there was a sense of relief too, as though the locals could now drop the pretence and go back to being themselves.

In one of the few bars still open Philip met a German woman, older than him, in her forties maybe with short hair the colour of corn. She told him that she, too, was an artist. In oils. Had a house in the village but used it rarely, as a base only, preferring to make the world her home. She'd just left New York where she'd had an exhibition of her paintings in a SoHo gallery. They were simple abstracts, had sold well, the Americans liking the boldness of their colours, their frankness.

She was like her paintings.

"My name is Frida," she said. "Come and dine with me, Tonight, yes? Bring wine, anything as long as it's red."

He obeyed.

They ate at a table that was a slab of marble, by candlelight, her three Saluki dogs lying sprawled on the black and white tiled floor. She wore a caftan and earrings that hung like fuchsias from her ear lobes, talked of her life, her friends, her lovers.

He said little, content just to be there, enjoying her eccentricity, the spacious comfort of her house. He was drinking too much he knew, but didn't care. This was what he wanted, this world, not the dull conventional life he lived back home. He closed his eyes and fell asleep stretched out on her white leather sofa, not moving once during the night.

Next morning she woke him with coffee. Outside the wind was strong, it battered the shutters, bent the trees; he thought he could hear the sea crashing onto the rocks. Sipping the bitter black liquid he recalled breakfasts in bed with Gail, herb teas, toast and honey, sticky fingers. Her sweet smile. He was missing her more than he'd expected, more than he'd ever admit of course.

Frida had just emerged from the shower when he came to her, took the towel from her hands, pulled her glistening body against his. Her curves, her skin, the very smell of her, exotic like some oriental flower, everything so unfamiliar and exciting. His lips found hers. It was an exorcism, a way of banishing ghosts, the past. He knew it was the right thing to do, right for him, and she wanted it too. It was the only thing.

And it worked.

It was instant, his infatuation with his woman, so very different from anyone he'd known. The way she spoke, direct, uncomplicated, confident, yet so very grateful when he came running to her cries the day the dogs cornered a cat. When he managed to scoop it up, holding its quivering body tight, she'd hugged his neck, whispered to him in German, eyes pressed tightly shut. Then there was her generosity with money, time, advice, anything Philip could ask for.

"I knew we'd be lovers that day we met" she said. "Within ten minutes. We share so much, our work, our attitude to life. Our need for adventure. It's true, yes?"

Even so he declined to move into her house and kept on his room. Inspired by her enthusiasm, her love of her work, he spent his days walking in the mountains above the village, stopping to sketch things that caught his eye, a hut inhabited by goats, rock formations, clouds like sheep flocking overhead. Or he would crouch besides a clump of greenery, intent on capturing every detail with his pen. Afterwards he'd stop at a bar, eat bread and olives, drink the local red wine.

As the sky darkened he would go back to his room, tired, his feet heavy. Would flop onto his bed, lie there watching a spider on the ceiling, maybe even sleep for a while. Later he would go to Frida.

For two, three weeks he sent no postcards. There was nothing he wanted to say, nothing he could squeeze onto a postcard. Besides, he hadn't heard from Gail. Not a word. Unexpectedly he found it irritating, her silence, the fact that she felt no need to communicate with him. What was she doing with her time, for god's sake? Was she missing him?

Frida sensed something. She put wood on the *stufa*, filling the room with the rich smell of pine wood. Sat at his knee, curling her long legs under her. The wind howled; the dogs twitched in their sleep.

"It's time you went home," she said. "Italy is finished for you, for now anyway. Soon you and I will be finished. Better to part now."

"Hey, no, no, no." He pulled her close. "Don't say that. You're so wrong."

He kissed the back of her neck. She didn't turn to him.

Later, alone, he knew she was right. But still he put off the decision to leave, to book a flight. He'd go when he'd finished another dozen sketches. When the last leaves had fallen from the trees. When his money ran out. Besides, he loved the village as it was now: slow, empty almost except for the locals, familiar faces on bodies now plump with sweaters and cardigans. Their lives were now reduced to eating, sleeping, a little work, not much. And waiting for spring.

It rained for days on end.

Then one day, Frida left. Bolting the shutters, slamming the door, she came down the steps to her car sheltering under a huge sun umbrella. Philip stood close to her, though he was already soaked to the skin.

"Why are you going? Couldn't you stay a little longer?"

"I told you. It's time."

"Where are you going?"

"Vienna. I'm meeting someone."

She climbed into the car, shuffled the luggage to make more space for the dogs. She pressed a button and the window slid silently down.

"Why don't you come with me?"

"Because...you're meeting someone?"

"I don't have to."

He sighed.

"I'd love to." He sighed. "Really I would. But no."

It would never work, their relationship would last no time, was already past its best, hanging on by a thread. Like the fat green marrows he'd sketched, hung over a wall, the stems yellow and rotting.

She blew him a kiss, started the engine and pulled away up the narrow road.

Still he was sorry to see her go. She was a lifeline.

And now he was really alone. Walking empty streets, sitting in silent bars, gazing through the rain-striped window of his room, his mind returned again and again to home. To Gail. To what he could be doing if he were with her. He missed his little attic studio, hardly more than a box room, but big enough. He missed his work, his friends. This, the time he'd spent in Italy, had been like stepping into a parallel world. But it wasn't real. It was a game. Much as he'd like to belong here, he didn't. Much as he'd like to be self-sufficient, he wasn't. He needed someone to care for, someone to care for him.

He wrote another postcard: WISH YOU WERE HERE. A cliché, but appropriate.

He didn't send it.

Instead, next morning, before the weak sun had risen over the village, he packed his belongings, said goodbye to his room, his landlord. He was going home.

It was late when he arrived back at the house. He'd rung to ask Gail if she'd collect him from the station – he'd tried at least half a dozen times – but there was no reply. In the end he'd taken a taxi, emptying his pockets to pay for it. There was no light on in the house.

For a moment his heart stopped. Had something happened? One of her parents taken ill maybe, or had she had an accident herself? Of course, no-one would have known how to contact him. He should have left his details. He was stupid.

What if she was trapped in the house, alone, terrified?

The key was in its usual place, under a pot of now dead chrysanthemums. As he put the key in the lock and turned it, his hand trembled.

"Gail? Where are you? I'm back?"

He knew at once that the house was empty, had been for a while. It felt not just cold, but somehow hollow. He switched on the kitchen light. Everything was neat, clean, dishes put away. That was Gail, always tidying up.

Propped against the kettle was a postcard, one of the ones that Gail had bought to help raise funds for a local cat charity. Reluctantly he picked it up.

HATE TO ADMIT IT BUT YOU WERE RIGHT, PHIL, BEING ALONE HAS HELPED ME REALISE I'M NOT READY FOR COMMITMENT YET. IN FACT I'VE REALLY ENJOYED BEING SINGLE AGAIN, AS I'M SURE YOU HAVE. SO TIME TO CALL IT A DAY I THINK, DON'T YOU? LET ME KNOW WHEN YOU'RE BACK SO WE CAN SORT OUT WHAT TO DO ABOUT THE HOUSE, ETC. LOVE, GAIL.

There was a single kiss. And a PS squeezed up the side. THERE'S SOME OF YOUR FAVOURITE CHOCOLATE ICE CREAM TO BE FINISHED IN THE FREEZER.

He turned the card over. Two fat ginger cats wearing pink straw hats stared out at him. Were they smirking or was he imagining it?

FOR THE LAST TIME

They put out the red flags. At least, they decorated the entrance to the hotel, her room, the one she always had, her corner table with a profusion of red gladioli. Her favourite flowers, as flamboyant as she was. Had once been anyway. One of the few flowers that grew well in southern Italy.

Tears filled her gooseberry eyes.

"Everyone is so kind," she cried, hobbling into reception and the outstretched arms of the manager.

"*Benvenuto, cara signora.*" He kissed her on each cheek, her skin brown and shiny, like polished wood. She smelt of the strawberry flavoured, strawberry coloured lipstick with which she plumped up lips that had shrivelled to a straight line over the years.

Once men had been drawn to those lips. Three husbands, she'd had. And more lovers than anyone knew, even she herself had lost count. Still, at eighty three she was an attractive woman.

"We are so happy to welcome you back, *Signora*. Truly."

Time and again, over some fifty years, she'd returned to the same resort, the same hotel, the indulgence of not having to find her way around, go sightseeing with the masses, speak any more than a smattering of Italian interspersed with English. *Meta e meta,* she called it. Half and half. The locals were used to it, understood what she said first time, most of it anyway. In her dotage she'd been drawn back even more often to the sun, the sea. The past. Memories were everywhere.

Two husbands and three lovers had accompanied her, at different times of course.

"This" she would tell them "is Ernesto. I knew him when he was hardly more than a boy."

The swarthy man, middle aged now, would stand to attention, hands folded neat as a napkin beneath his pasta paunch. Would smile politely.

She forgot, or chose not to mention, that she had been the woman who had initiated him into sex, had taken him one stormy night to her room and bed, touching his firm young body, smooth as butter, with knowing fingers until he writhed with delight, moaned, discovered even more pleasures awaiting him as she pulled him towards her.

Or it would be Umberto she introduced. Or Sergio. Or Ottavio.

She was something of a celebrity in the village. Notorious even. *Lei e una donna sexy*, they said of her, with a mixture of admiration and condemnation. The local girls had much to thank her for.

But now she was here for the last time.

"I know it," she told the head waiter as she twirled spaghetti round her fork slowly, carefully, bent low over her plate and sucked the long, white strands into her mouth. She chewed, swallowed, dabbed with a napkin.

"I feel it in my bones. In my veins. My blood moves so slowly these days, no more than a trickle. My heart misses beats altogether. My pulse... well, I haven't got one. Here, feel. My body is grinding to a halt, and there's nothing I can do to get it going again."

She sipped wine noisily.

"Yes, this year will be my last."

"*Ma signora*, you must not talk this way. You are still a strong woman, you have much life in you. Please, I beg you, don't say these things."

Diners at nearby tables, disturbed by the agitation in his voice, twisted in their chairs to watch as the old lady plucked at the head waiter's sleeve with sharp fingers, whispered loudly as those who are deaf often do.

"Please my dear, don't upset yourself. What's there to fear? It seems to me that dying is just another change, a new beginning. And if I'm wrong and it's an end, then that's that. No, I'm not going to upset myself, so don't you."

She edged back in her seat, sucked her teeth, belched. Suddenly she smiled.

"What I am going to do is make the very most of my last time here. Bring me champagne!"

She invited the waiters to share it with her, sat on in the empty dining room surrounded by young men in white jackets who jostled each other, joked in dialect, were shy and attentive at the same time. Through the panoramic windows the night sky could be seen, fizzy with stars, and below, the village streets, shops still open, ribbons of coloured lights, knots of people.

"I shall die happy," said the old lady.

Next day they took her down to the beach, settled her onto a chair under a red and yellow striped umbrella, covered her feet so that her ankles wouldn't swell. Closing her eyes she recalled when she'd had no need of protection, had stretched flat out on the sand and felt the sun's scorching rays turn her from one shade of brown to another, each more beautiful. She'd tanned easy as a pie in an oven. It was her gypsy blood, they said. Her father had taken to the road when she was so small she could barely clamber onto a chair to wave him goodbye. She hardly remembered him, no more than the smell of the cigarettes he was forever rolling, of his shirts drying on the back of chairs by the fire; occasional raised voices and slammed doors.

Mind you, she'd always worn a swimming costume. Nowadays girls sunbathed naked and brazen, had hardly any proof that they'd changed colour at all. She had been proud of the whiteness of her breasts, had known it to be tantalising, the moon sickle of white above a clinging bodice. Like a subtle invitation.

Closing her eyes she recalled the first man in her life, her first husband. An artist. Artist friends had told him about the village; he came for inspiration, brought an easel, paints, an eye for detail that was to make him famous, later. She came to keep him company, had been at once entranced by the heat, the quiet, by wine that tasted of earth and warm rains. In love with it all she flirted with everyone, for no reason other than that they were part of it, they belonged. He, her husband, had been jealous. As though to assert himself he had made love to her again and again, in the mornings, before dinner, during the night waking her from sleep.

When she got back to England it had been confirmed. After five years of trying, she was at last pregnant.

Since then she'd borne six children, all slipping from her with the ease of stones from plums, all golden skinned with eyes the colour of April skies. One had died within a year. Two had become businessmen, successful, with thatched cottages in the commuter belt, daily help, ponies for the children. The one daughter, a twin, had settled into the role of wife and mother without a thought, her domesticity disappointing the old lady.

The last two were her favourites. The other twin, a musician who made the flute sound sweet as wind chimes. And the youngest, a gypsy who had wandered off many years ago and never returned, sending instead letters written on the banks of yellow rivers where elephants hauled logs and clouds of mosquitoes threatened like rain, or from Times Square beneath the cigarette advertisement that puffs real smoke, or a Mexican bar. Places she'd longed to see for herself. Now she saw them through him; it was a good second best.

Closing her eyes, she slept.

And then there was the bar, Gino's, where she'd spent so many hours beneath the spinning fan sipping drinks with names she couldn't pronounce, tastes she couldn't recognise, but that made her feel good just the same. Her doctor, before she left, had warned her against alcohol. Also sugar. Also rich pastries, seafood which might be contaminated, garlic sauces. Against everything she enjoyed, it seemed.

"*Ah signora.*" Gino wiped his hands on his apron, came out from behind the counter, arms wide in welcome. His joy was genuine.

"And what you want? Your usual?"

He took pride in remembering what customers drank. She couldn't upset him by ordering a cappuccino. Besides, she didn't really want one. Accepting the generous gin and tonic, she ignored the dish of olives, finding them too bitter now, pushed aside the nuts she'd have loved to eat but daren't, not with her teeth being crumbly as biscuits.

It was awful getting old, she decided again. Simply dreadful.

People crushed in for their pre-dinner drinks. Many of them recognised the old lady, shook her hand; a woman she couldn't recall at all hugged her warmly. One man, very old, maybe as old as she was, reminded her of someone. She was sure she knew him and yet, no, it wasn't possible. The man she remembered had been elderly years ago, would surely be buried in the cemetery up above the village by now, surrounded by Cypress trees and silence.

That day in the bar he'd not stopped talking, seducing her with his words, a wiry man with white hair, a single gold earring, eyes that glowed as though lit from within. Was he mad, she wondered, fascinated, drawn to his madness if such it was. He told her of his life up in the mountains, a hut he'd built himself, a half wild dog, some chickens. A poet, he said, needs to be away from people, needs space, emptiness. He told the legend of a musician who made love to a siren – only here, he added, touching his forehead – but even so his audacity caused an earthquake, and he fell into a ravine and was killed. *Una tragedia*, he said, his face unsmiling. She wondered if he had made it up on the spur of the moment, on her behalf, but didn't ask. It was a good story anyway.

He'd put his rough hand gently on her knee, leant forward. She could feel his breath.

"The most important thing in life," he said "is love."

There had been many times when she would have agreed with him. Not now though. Now she wanted most of all to be able to dance. Music came from somewhere outside on the street, a guitar, drums, music full of bounce and energy that made your foot twitch, made you smile.

She'd been a champion ballroom dancer once, with husband number two; had spent patient hours stitching sequins onto swirling skirts that would flash and wink as she whirled across floors slippery as ice, her head dipping this way and that. She'd been slim then, light on her feet. Like a bird of paradise, a reporter on a local paper had written. She had cups to prove it.

Now all she could manage was to tap the table with her fingers, and even that hurt. Nothing the doctors could do about arthritis. She was growing twisted and gnarled as an old tree. It made her furious though she wasn't sure what at. God? Her own body for being so weak? The unfairness of old age?

He'd died, that husband, in a freak accident at the bus garage where he worked, a tyre bursting and throwing him against a steel rod that had gone into his back, pierced his lungs. For half an hour, as they waited for an ambulance to arrive, he'd chatted, joked even. He died before he reached the hospital.

She'd never found a dancing partner to compare with him, though you had to admit the Italians did their best to put romance back onto the dance floor. They held you so close you could feel the keys in their pocket, she'd say.

"I won't be back," she told Gino. "This is my last time. I'm dying."

He protested, raised sombre eyes, his hands clasped as though in prayer. She took no notice. She tipped her head to one side.

"The only way you'll see me again is if I decide to haunt you."

He insisted she have another drink, free, whatever she wanted. Asked if he might join her at the table.

"*Non credo questo, non e possibile,*" he muttered, shaking his head. He drank thirstily. She was an old friend, a good one. He'd miss her. His father had confessed to him that he'd had an affair with her once, a few torrid nights of passion that he'd never forgotten. She could almost be Gino's mother.

She found his concern flattering; it was taking years off her, all this attention.

At night she took sleeping pills to stop thoughts, memories, one or two regrets tumbling around in her head like dice in a cup. Yet still she dreamed of a time when men had fluttered around her like the moths that battered themselves against the windows, unable to resist the light. She liked the light on at night, in case she woke. In case she couldn't remember where she was, as sometimes happened. And then she'd panic and call for someone, anyone, to catch her and haul her back from the edge of the precipice.

In the mornings she ate hearty breakfasts.

She wrote postcards to people, the few whose addresses she could remember, though then she often missed vital details.

It's lovely to be here again, like coming home. Sad to know I'll never see it again. Will I even see you, I wonder? Love.

On the street one day a boy stopped and stared at her, a child of maybe seven or eight, with black curly hair, his mouth slightly open as though in amazement. Maybe he was a little frightened, too, but covered it when he caught her eye by winking boldly. She winked back. He couldn't keep his eyes off her with her bright purple dress, her dyed red hair, her walking stick.

She waved it at him, beckoned, rummaged in her bag.

"*Ecco.*" She offered him chocolates, dark squares wrapped in silver paper. He hesitated, snatched them, drew back. Silently he unwrapped and ate them as he followed her cautious progress along the narrow pavement. Overhead grapevines hung heavy with small, hard berries. He jumped up, tore off a bunch, pelted her with them. Then stood waiting. She turned, stared back, reached for a bunch hanging close to the wall and flung it at him, amazed when it actually hit his shoulder. A pause, then they both laughed.

After that the boy was never far from the old lady. Scruffy in his torn T-shirt, fraying cut off trousers, his bare feet grey with dust, he made up for it with his huge eyes, deceptively innocent expression, his laughter that bubbled up like the Coca Cola he never stopped drinking. It cost her a fortune, but she didn't mind. At first they held conversations of a sort, using their hands, their faces, but soon they lapsed into a silent understanding, any kind of conversation being superfluous. They had the same simplistic outlook on life, shared not just an ability to live in the present moment, but also a love of ice cream, especially pistachio. Sitting side by side on a wall overlooking the beach, shaded by a carob tree, surrounded by the sound of voices, laughter, the boy's sticky hand in hers, the old lady knew that this was a very special moment.

"You" she told him "will be my last Italian boyfriend." He grinned. He grinned at whatever she said.

And suddenly it was time to go home. There was a celebration dinner, all her favourite dishes: *spaghetti alle vongole, osso buco*, fennel and *radicchio* salad, creamy *zabaglione* for dessert. The cook emerged hot and red faced from the kitchen between each course.

"You like?" he would ask anxiously. "Is good?"

"*Si, si*" she assured him, eating every last morsel. It was very good.

She took indigestion tablets before she went to bed but still awoke with palpitations, a pain in her chest as though someone was kneeling on it. She was sweating.

"This is it, my time has come," she muttered, fumbling frantically in the dark for the bedside telephone, trying to remember Italian for doctor or help. Or, I am dying.

In the morning she was right as rain.

There were tears from some of the staff, old timers she'd known for years; others were blinked back. The boy stood quietly behind a forest of legs, too timid to push his way through, until she bent and held out her arms. He ran into them.

"*Cara, cara signora*. You will be sadly missed." The manager handed her a single white rose.

As the taxi set off for the airport, it drove slowly through the village streets. Seeing her sitting there so upright in her bright blue hat, people waved, many she didn't know, but she waved back. Her subjects were paying their last respects. It was wonderful, and yet sad too. And so tiring. She sank back in her seat and fell asleep at once. The driver, peering into his mirror, worried that she might indeed have slipped away. But no, she made it safely back to England, to a chilly grey summer and an even bleaker winter of rising prices and coal strikes and muggings on streets she'd known all her life, known and loved to walk. She grew feebler, slower, even more prone to falling asleep in odd places. Life really was too much effort.

And yet.

In the spring she revived a little. She drank tonic wine, ate a salad a day, took vitamin pills. The sun shone anaemically and she thought of Italy, a different sun, warmer, more virile, and of the way she felt when she was there. More alive.

"Yes," she decided. "I'll go back again, just once more. For the very last time."

The travel agent made the booking that same afternoon.

THE END
La fine

MISSING ITALY?

LIKE TO GO BACK... AND EVEN FURTHER BACK IN TIME?

STONES OF THE MADONNA
Jan Mazzoni

They lay on a lace doily on top of the tallboy,
three small stones, each one pierced as though
it had been run through with a spear.
She'd polished them until they gleamed like pearls;
they had a smell about them of deep oceans and green fronds.
They had powers.

It's 1939 and Lily and her American doctor husband James have come to the Amalfi coast in southern Italy in search of a new start. And how could they not be happy in a place where the scenery is stunning, the locals generous and welcoming, where the air is filled with the fragrance of jasmine and the laughter of children?

But escaping the past isn't so easy.

In the sultry silence of one of the hottest summers for years Lily discovers things about herself that she never knew. She discovers things about James too, things she'd sooner not know. And though the chill and looming shadow of war edges closer and closer, ultimately it is not the war that poses the biggest threat to Lily's new-found contentment...

Printed in Poland
by Amazon Fulfillment
Poland Sp. z o.o., Wrocław